Günter Grass

Crabwalk

Translated from the German by Krishna Winston

Harcourt, Inc.
Orlando   Austin   New York   San Diego   Toronto   London

A Reading Group Guide is available at www.HarcourtBooks.com

This is a translation of *Im Krebsgang*

Library of Congress Cataloging-in-Publication Data
Grass, Günter, 1927–
[Im Krebsgang. English]
Crabwalk/by Günter Grass; translated from the German
by Krishna Winston.
p.   cm.
ISBN 0-15-100764-0
I. Winston, Krishna.   II. Title.
PT2613.R338 I413 2002
833'.914—dc21   2002013205

Text set in Granjon
Designed by Cathy Riggs

Printed in the United States of America

First U.S. edition

A C E G I K J H F D B

in memoriam

I

"WHY ONLY NOW?" HE SAYS, THIS PERSON NOT TO be confused with me. Well, because Mother's incessant nagging... Because I wanted to cry the way I did at the time, when the cry spread across the water, but couldn't anymore... Because for the true story... hardly more than three lines... Because only now...

The words still don't come easily. This person, who doesn't like excuses, reminds me that I'm a professional: had a way with words at a young age, signed on as a cub reporter with one of the Springer tabloids, soon had the lingo down pat, then switched over to the *Tageszeitung,* where Springer was the favorite whipping boy, later kept it short and sweet as a mercenary for various news agencies, and eventually freelanced for a while, chopping and shredding all sorts of subjects to be served up as articles: something new every day. The news of the day.

True enough, I said. But that's about all I know how to do. If I really have to settle my own historical accounts now, everything I messed up is going to be ascribed to the sinking of a ship. Why? Because Mother was nine months pregnant when it happened, because it's sheer coincidence that I'm alive.

And already, again, I'm doing someone else's bidding, but at least I can leave myself out of it for the time being, because this story began long before me, more than a hundred years ago, in Schwerin, the ducal seat of Mecklenburg, nestled amid seven lakes, priding itself on postcards of its Schelfstadt district and a castle bristling with turrets, and outwardly left unharmed by the wars.

Initially I didn't think a provincial burg that history had crossed off long ago could attract anyone besides tourists, but then the starting place for my story suddenly acquired a presence on the Internet. An anonymous source was posting biographical information, complete with dates, street names, and report cards, a treasure trove for someone like me who was under pressure to dig up the past.

I'd bought myself a Mac, with a modem, as soon as these things came on the market. For my work I need to be able to snare information wherever it may be wandering around the world. I got pretty good at using the computer. Soon terms like *browser* and *hyperlink* were no longer Chinese to me. With a click of the mouse I could haul in stuff that I might use or might end up throwing in the trash. Soon, out of idleness or inclination, I began flitting from chat room to chat room, also responded to the most idiotic spam, checked out a couple of porno sites, and after some aimless surfing finally landed on sites where old unregenerates but also freshly minted neo-Nazis were venting their venom on hate pages. And suddenly—entering the name of a ship as a keyword—I clicked my way to the right address: www.blutzeuge.de. In Gothic script the "Comrades of Schwerin" were strutting their stuff. Something about a martyr. Dredging up the past. More ludicrous than disgusting.

In the meantime it's become clear which martyr is meant and what he's supposed to have shed his blood for. But I'm still not sure how to go about this: should I do as I was taught and unpack one life at a time, in order, or do I have to sneak up on time in a crabwalk, seeming to go backward but actually scuttling sideways, and thereby working my way forward fairly rapidly? Only this much is certain: Nature, or to be more precise, the Baltic, said yea and amen more than half a century ago to everything that will have to be reported here.

First comes a person whose gravestone was smashed. After getting through school—the commercial track—he apprenticed at a bank, finishing up without attracting undue attention. Not a word about this phase on the Internet. On the Web site dedicated to Wilhelm Gustloff, born in Schwerin in 1895, he was celebrated as "the martyr." The site did not mention the problems with his larynx, the chronic weakness of the lungs that prevented him from proving his bravery in the First World War. While Hans Castorp, a young man from a good Hanseatic family, received orders from his creator to leave the Magic Mountain, and on page 994 of the novel was left to fall as a volunteer on Flanders Field or to escape into a literary no-man's-land, in 1917 the Schwerin Life Insurance Bank took the precaution of shipping its industrious employee off to Davos in Switzerland, where he was supposed to recover from his illness. That locale's remarkable air restored his health so completely that death could get at him only in another form; for the time being, he did not care to return to Schwerin and its lowland climate.

Wilhelm Gustloff found a job as an assistant in an observatory. When this research station was converted into a Helvetian foundation, he was promoted to recording secretary of the observatory, a post that gave him time to supplement his income by working as a door-to-door salesman for a company that offered household insurance. Through his moonlighting, he became familiar with all the Swiss cantons. Meanwhile his wife Hedwig was not idle either; as a secretary in the office of an attorney named Moses Silberroth, she did her job without experiencing any sense of dissonance with her Aryan loyalties.

Up to this point, the facts offer a composite portrait of a solid bourgeois couple. But, as will become apparent, the Gustloffs' way of life merely appeared to be consistent with Swiss notions of gainful employment. Secretly at first, later openly—and for a long time with his employer's tacit approval—the observatory secretary exercised his inborn organizational talent: he joined the Nazi Party, and by early '36 had recruited about five thousand new members among German and Austrian citizens living in Switzerland, had established local chapters all over the country, and had had the new members pledge their loyalty to someone whom Providence had thought up as the Führer.

Gustloff himself had been appointed Landesgruppenleiter by Gregor Strasser, the man in charge of Party organization. Strasser belonged to the left wing of the Party, and two years after resigning all his posts in '32 to protest his Führer's cozy relationship with industry, he was included in the Röhm Putsch and liquidated by his own people; his brother Otto saved his own skin by fleeing Germany. At that point Gustloff had to find someone else to emulate.

On the basis of a question posed in the Graubünden cantonal parliament, an officer from the Swiss Aliens Police interrogated Gustloff as to how he envisioned carrying out his duties as NSDAP Landesgruppenleiter in the Helvetian Confederation. He is said to have replied, "In all the world, I love my wife and my mother most. If my Führer ordered me to kill them, I would obey him."

On the Internet this quotation was challenged as apocryphal. In the chat room sponsored by the Comrades of Schwerin, this and other lies were characterized as fabrications by the Jewish writer Emil Ludwig. It was claimed that, on the contrary, the influence of Gregor Strasser on the martyr had remained in force. Gustloff had always put the socialist element in his worldview ahead of the nationalist element. Soon battles raged between the right and left wings of the chatters. A virtual Night of the Long Knives took its toll.

But then all interested users were reminded of a date

that allegedly proved that the hand of Providence had been at work. Something I had tried to explain away as a mere coincidence elevated the Party functionary Gustloff to a participant in a celestial design: on 30 January 1945, fifty years to the day after the martyr's birth, the ship named after him began to sink, signaling the downfall of the Thousand-Year Reich, twelve years — again to the day — since the Nazis' seizure of power.

There it stands, as if hewn into granite, that damned date on which everything began, later to escalate murderously, reach a climax, come to an end. I, too, thanks to Mother, began on that repeatedly unlucky day. She, however, lives by a different calendar, and grants no power to coincidence or any similarly blanket explanation.

"Don't get me wrong!" exclaims this woman, whom I never refer to possessively as "my mother" but only as "Mother." "That ship could've been named after anyone, and it still would've gone down. What I'd like to know is, what was that Russki thinking of when he gave orders to shoot them three whatchamacallums straight at us...?"

She still rambles on this way, as if buckets of time hadn't flowed over the dam since then. Trampling her words to death, putting sentences through the wringer. In her idiom, potatoes are *bullwen,* cottage cheese is *glumse,* and when she cooks cod in a mustard sauce, she calls it *pomuchel.* In typical Low German fashion, she also pronounces most *g*'s like *y*'s. Mother's parents, August and Erna Pokriefke, came from the area known as the

Koschneiderei, and were referred to as Koshnavians. She, however, grew up in Langfuhr. She considers herself a product not of Danzig but of this elongated suburb, which kept expanding into the open countryside. One of its streets was Elsenstrasse, and to the child Ursula, who went by Tulla, it must have been all that was needed in the way of a world. When Mother talks about "way back when," even though she often recalls pleasant days on the nearby Baltic beaches or winter sleigh rides in the forests to the south of the suburb, she usually draws her listeners into the courtyard of the apartment house at 19 Elsenstrasse, and from there, past Harras, the chained German shepherd, into a carpentry shop, filled with the sounds of the circular saw, the band saw, the lathe, the planer, and the whining finishing machine. "When I was just a little brat, they let me stir the glue pot..." Which explains why, as the story goes, wherever she stood, lay, walked, ran, or cowered in a corner, the child Tulla had that legendary smell of carpenter's glue clinging to her.

It was thus not surprising that when they housed us in Schwerin right after the war, Mother decided to train as a carpenter in the Schelfstadt district. As a "resettler," the term used in the East, she was promptly assigned an apprenticeship with a master carpenter whose shack, with its four workbenches and constantly bubbling glue pot, was considered long established. From there it was not far to Lehmstrasse, where Mother and I had a tar-paper roof over our heads. If we hadn't gone ashore in Kolberg after the disaster, if the torpedo boat *Löwe* had brought us instead to Travemünde or Kiel, in the West, that is, as a "refugee from the East," as they called it over there, Mother would certainly have done an apprenticeship in carpentry, too. I consider it a coincidence, whereas from the first day she viewed the place where we were compulsorily placed as preordained.

"And when did that Russki, the captain of the U-boat, I mean, have his birthday? You're the one who usually knows that kind of thing..."

No, in this case I don't have as much information as about Wilhelm Gustloff, which I got off the Internet. All I could find online was the year of the Russian's birth and a few other facts and conjectures, the stuff journalists call background.

Aleksandr Marinesko was born in 1913, in the port of Odessa, on the Black Sea. The city must have been magnificent at one time, as the black-and-white images in the film *Battleship Potemkin* demonstrate. His mother came from Ukraine. His father was a Romanian, and had signed his papers "Marinescu" before he was condemned to death for mutiny. He managed to flee at the last minute.

His son Aleksandr grew up near the docks. And because Russians, Ukrainians, and Romanians, Greeks and Bulgarians, Turks and Armenians, Gypsies and Jews all lived there cheek by jowl, he spoke a mishmash of many languages, but must have been understood by his youth gang. No matter how hard he tried later on to speak Russian, he never quite succeeded in purging his father's

Romanian curses from his Yiddish-seasoned Ukrainian. When he was already a ship's mate on a trading vessel, people laughed at his linguistic hodgepodge; but in later years many must have discovered that there was nothing to laugh about, no matter how comical the U-boat commander's orders may have sounded.

Let's rewind to an earlier period: at seven, young Aleksandr is said to have watched from the overseas pier as the last White Russian troops and the exhausted remnants of the British and French troops that had been sent into the fray fled Odessa. Not long after that he saw the Reds march in. Purges took place. Then the civil war was as good as over. And several years later, when foreign ships were allowed once more to dock in the harbor, the boy is supposed to have shown persistence and soon real skill at diving for the coins that elegantly dressed passengers tossed into the brackish water.

The trio is not yet complete. We are still missing one. It was his deed that set in motion something that would exert a powerful undertow, and prove unstoppable. Because he unwittingly transformed the man from Schwerin into the movement's martyr, and the youth from Odessa into the hero of the Baltic Red Banner Fleet, he will be on trial for all time to come. Greedy now, I extracted this and similar indictments from that Web site, which I always found by searching under the same phrase: "A Jew fired the shots..."

As I have meanwhile learned, a polemical work brought out by the Franz Eher publishing house, Munich,

1936, and written by Party member and official speaker Wolfgang Diewerge, made the charge less equivocally. The Comrades of Schwerin, following the irrefutable logic of insanity, could proclaim, more definitively than Diewerge was yet in a position to know, "Without the Jew, the greatest maritime disaster of all times would never have taken place in the navigation channel west of Stolpmünde, which had been swept for mines. The Jew was the one...It's all the Jew's fault..."

Certain facts could nonetheless be gleaned from the exchanges stirred up in the chat room, some in English, some in German. One of the chatters knew that not long after the war began Diewerge had become manager of the Reich radio station in Danzig, and another had information on his doings in the postwar period: as the crony of other Nazi bigwigs, such as Achenbach, who became a Free Democratic member of the Bundestag, Diewerge allegedly infiltrated the liberal party of Nordrhein-Westfalen. And a third chatter added that in the seventies the former Nazi propaganda expert ran a discreet donation-laundering operation for the Free Democrats, in Neuwied am Rhein. Finally, questions about the assassin of Davos rose above the din in the crowded chat room, and were shot down with sharp replies.

In 1909, four years before Marinesko was born and fourteen years after Gustloff was born, David Frankfurter came into the world in the West Slavonian town of Daruvar, the son of a rabbi. Hebrew and German were spoken in the home, and in school David learned to speak and write Serbo-Croatian, but he was also subjected to the hatred directed against Jews that was part of everyday life. His efforts to come to terms with it must have been futile, because he was constitutionally incapable of putting up a robust defense, and on the other hand he despised the very notion of accepting life as it was.

David Frankfurter had only one thing in common with Wilhelm Gustloff: as the latter was initially handicapped by weak lungs, the former suffered from childhood on from chronic osteomyelitis. But whereas Gustloff managed to overcome his illness by going to Davos, and served the Party diligently once his health was restored, the doctors could not help David. He underwent five operations, but without success: a hopeless case.

Perhaps it was because of his illness that he took up the study of medicine, which he did in Germany, on his family's advice. His father and grandfather before him had studied there. Apparently he had trouble concentrating, because he was always ailing, and he failed the preclinical examination as well as subsequent examinations. But Party member Diewerge asserted on the Internet, in contrast to the writer Ludwig, whom Diewerge insisted on calling "Emil Ludwig-Cohn," that the Jew Frankfurter had been not only a weakling but also a lazy and shiftless student, a dandy and chain-smoker who frittered away his father's money.

Then began—on that thrice-cursed date—the year of the Nazi takeover—recently celebrated on the Internet. In Frankfurt the chain-smoker David got a taste of what was in store for him and other students. He witnessed the burning of books by Jewish authors. Suddenly a Star of David appeared at his station in the laboratory. Hate, now taking a physical form, was closing in on him. He and others were pelted with insults by students raucously proclaiming their membership in the Aryan race. This he could not put up with. It was unbearable. He fled to Switzerland, continuing his studies in Berne, seemingly a safe haven—where he again failed to pass various examinations. Nonetheless he sent his parents cheery, even confident letters, wangling more money out of his father. When his mother died the following year, he gave up his studies. Perhaps in hopes of gaining support from relatives, he risked a trip back to the Reich, where he stood by without lifting a finger while his uncle, a rabbi like his father, had his reddish beard pulled on a street in Berlin by a young man who shouted, "Hepp, hepp, Jew!"

Any account along these lines can be found in *Murder in Davos,* a fictionalized version by the best-selling author Emil Ludwig, brought out in 1936 by Querido, a publishing house founded in Amsterdam by German émigrés. Again the Comrades of Schwerin had a different story on their Web site; they took the word of Party member Diewerge, because he quoted what the rabbi, Dr. Salomon Frankfurter, purportedly told the Berlin police when they interrogated him: "It is not true that an adolescent boy pulled me by my beard (which in point of fact is black, not red), shouting, 'Hepp, hepp, Jew!'"

I was unable to determine whether this police investigation, not ordered until two years after the alleged incident, employed any coercion. At any rate, David went back to Berne, and must have been in despair on a number of counts. For one thing, he was supposed to resume his studies, hitherto completely unsuccessful, and for another, to his chronic physical pain had been added grief over his mother's death. Furthermore, his impressions from his brief visit to Berlin became even more depressing when he read reports in the local and foreign newspapers about concentration camps in Oranienburg, Dachau, and elsewhere.

Suicidal thoughts must have come to him toward the end of '35, and repeatedly thereafter. Later, when the trial was under way, a psychological evaluation commissioned by the defense noted: "As a result of psychological factors of a personal nature, Frankfurter found himself in an untenable emotional situation, from which he felt he had to escape. His depression gave rise to the idea of suicide. But the instinct for self-preservation innate to every human being deflected the bullet from himself onto another victim."

The Internet carried no nit-picking commentaries on this evaluation. Nonetheless, I had a growing suspicion that what lurked behind the URL www.blutzeuge.de was no skinhead group calling itself the Comrades of Schwerin but a solitary clever young fanatic. Someone scuttling crabwise like me, sniffing for the scents and similar exudations of history.

A shiftless student? That was me, when I decided that German literature was too boring and media studies at the Otto Suhr Institute too theoretical.

Initially, when I left Schwerin and then migrated from East to West Berlin by S-Bahn, shortly before the Wall went up, I made a real effort, as I had promised Mother when we parted. Worked my tail off in school. Was sixteen and a half when I got my first whiff of freedom. Lived in Schmargendorf, near Roseneck, with Mother's old schoolmate Jenny, who had supposedly shared a bunch of crazy experiences with her. Had my own room, with a skylight. A nice time that was, actually.

Aunt Jenny's attic apartment on Karlsbader Strasse looked like a doll's house. Everywhere, on side tables and wall brackets, she had porcelain figurines under glass. Dancers in tutus on pointe. Some of them balancing in daring arabesques, all with delicate little heads and long necks. As a young woman, Jenny had been a ballerina, and quite well known, but then, during one of the many air raids that were reducing the Reich capital to rubble, both her feet were crushed, with the result that she hobbled when she brought me an assortment of snacks for afternoon tea, though her arm gestures remained fluid. And like the fragile figurines in her oh-so-sweet little attic, the small face atop her now gaunt but agile neck bore a smile that seemed frozen in place. She often had the shivers, and drank a good deal of hot lemonade.

I enjoyed living there. She pampered me. And when she talked about her old girlfriend—"My darling Tulla slipped a note to me a little while ago"—I would be tempted for a few minutes to feel some fondness for Mother, that tough old bitch; but soon she would get on my nerves again. The messages she managed to smuggle out of Schwerin to Karlsbader Strasse bristled with admonitions, underlined to the point of no contradiction and intended to "pester" me into compliance, to use Mother's word: "The boy's got to study, study, study. That's the only reason why I sent him to the West—so he could amount to something..."

As I read that, I could hear the words Mother would have used in her native Langfuhr idiom: "That's all I live for—so's my son can bear witness one of these days." Speaking for her girlfriend, Aunt Jenny would admonish me, too, in her gentle but pointed tone. I had no choice but to work my tail off in school.

My class included a bunch of other kids who'd escaped from the East. I had a lot of catching up to do on subjects such as democracy and the rule of law. In addition to English I had to take French—Russian was a thing of the past. I also began to see how capitalism worked, the whole business of structural unemployment. I was no star, but I passed the university entrance exams, as Mother had demanded.

In other respects I held my own, when it came to girls, for instance, and didn't even have to pinch pennies, because when I went over to the enemy of the working class, with her blessing, Mother slipped me another address in the West: "This guy's your father, or could be. A cousin of mine. He knocked me up shortly before he had to go in the service. That's what he thinks. Send him a note to let him know how you're doing, once you're settled over there..."

———

Comparisons are odious. Yet where finances were concerned, I soon found myself in the same situation as David Frankfurter in Berne, whose distant father deposited a tidy sum in his Swiss bank account every month. Mother's cousin Harry Liebenau—God rest his soul—was the son of the master carpenter back on Elsenstrasse, and had been living in Baden-Baden since the late fifties. As the cultural editor for Southwest German Radio, he was responsible for late-night programming: poetry around midnight, when only the pines in the Black Forest were still listening.

Since I didn't want to be hitting up Mother's girlfriend for money all the time, I fired off a rather nice letter, if I do say so myself, and after the closing flourish, "Your unknown son," I made sure to include my bank account number, in my most legible handwriting. Apparently he was too happily married to write back, but every month without fail he came through with far more than the minimum child support, the sum of two hundred marks, a small fortune at the time. Aunt Jenny knew nothing about this arrangement, but apparently she had been acquainted with Mother's cousin Harry, if only fleetingly, as she let on rather than actually said, a faint flush coloring her doll's face.

In early '67, not long after I had extricated myself from Karlsbader Strasse and moved to Kreuzberg, where I soon dropped my studies and clambered aboard at Springer's *Morgenpost* as a cub reporter, the money supply dried up. From then on I never wrote to my sugar daddy, or at most a Christmas card. Why should I have? In one of her smuggled messages, Mother had made it clear how things stood: "No need to fall all over yourself thanking him. He knows well enough why he has to pay up..."

She couldn't write to me openly, because by now she had become the head of a carpentry brigade in a large state-owned plant that produced bedroom furniture on the Five-Year Plan. As a Party member, she could not have contacts in the West, and certainly not with her son, a GDR deserter who was writing for the capitalist propaganda press, first short pieces, then longer ones, taking aim at a Communist system that couldn't hold its own without walls and barbed wire; that created problems enough for her.

I assumed that Mother's cousin had cut me off because I was writing for Springer's tabloids instead of finishing my studies. He was right, too, in a way, the frigging liberal. And soon after the attack on Rudi Dutschke, I said good-bye to Springer. Kept pretty much to the left from then on. Wrote for a bunch of halfway progressive papers next, because there was a lot going on at the time, and kept my head above water fairly well, even without three times the minimum child support. Herr Liebenau wasn't my real father anyway. Mother had just used him as a stand-in. It was from her that I learned, later on, that the director of midnight programming died of heart failure in the late seventies, before I was even married. He was about Mother's age, a little past fifty.

As substitutes she offered me the names of various other men, who, she said, should be considered possible father candidates. One of them, who disappeared, was supposedly called Joachim or Jochen, and another, older one, who allegedly poisoned the watchdog Harras, was Walter.

No, I never did have a proper father, just interchangeable phantoms. In that respect the three heroes I've been instructed to focus on were better off. It's clear, at any rate, that Mother really had no idea by whom she was pregnant when she set out on that morning of 30 January 1945 with her parents, leaving the Gotenhafen-Oxhöft pier as passenger number seven thousand such-and-such. The man for whom the ship had been named could identify a businessman, Hermann Gustloff, as his father. And as a boy in Odessa, the man who succeeded in sinking the overcrowded ship had received fairly regular beatings from Papa Marinesko—tangible proof of paternal solicitude—for belonging to a band of thieves, reportedly known as *blatnye*. And David Frankfurter, who traveled from Berne to Davos to set in motion the process by which the ship came to be named for a martyr, had an honest-to-goodness rabbi as his father. Even I, fatherless though I was, would eventually become a father.

What would he have smoked? Junos, those famously round cigarettes? Or flat Orients? Maybe the fashionable ones with gold tips? There are no photos of him smoking, except a newspaper picture from the late sixties that shows him with a glow stuck in his mouth during the brief stopover in Switzerland that he was finally allowed to make as an older gentleman, his civil service career soon to be behind him. Anyway, he puffed away constantly, like me, and for that reason took a seat in a smoking car of the Swiss National Railway.

Both of them traveled by train. Around the time that David Frankfurter was making his way from Berne to Davos, Wilhelm Gustloff was on the road organizing. In the course of his trip he visited several local chapters of the Nazi Party, and established new troops of the Hitler Youth and the BDM, the League of German Girls. Because this trip took place at the end of January, he no doubt gave speeches in Berne and Zurich, Glarus and Zug, marking the third anniversary of the takeover, speeches enthusiastically received by audiences of Germans and Austrians abroad. Since his employer, the observatory, succumbing to pressure from Social Democratic deputies, had relieved him of his post the previous year, he had complete control over his schedule. Although there were numerous Swiss demonstrations against his activities as an agitator—leftist papers called him "the dictator of Davos"—and a national MP named Bringolf demanded his expulsion, in the canton of Graubünden and throughout the Swiss confederation he also found plenty of politicians and officials who supported him, and not only financially. In Davos the management of the resort saw to it that he regularly received the lists of newly arrived guests, whereupon he would get in touch with those who were German citizens, not merely inviting but summoning them to Party events; unexcused absences were recorded and the names passed on to the appropriate offices in the Reich.

Around the time the smoking student took his train trip, having asked for a one-way ticket in Berne, and the martyr-to-be was proving himself in the service of his party, ship's mate Aleksandr Marinesko had already switched from the merchant marine to the Black Sea Red Banner Fleet, in whose training division he received instruction in navigation and was then groomed to be a U-boat helmsman. At the same time he belonged to the Komsomol youth organization and turned out to be a formidable off-duty drinker—for which he compensated with particular diligence while on duty; on board he never touched a drop. Soon Marinesko was assigned to a U-boat, the *SC-306 Piksja,* as navigational officer; after the war began, this unit of the fleet, only recently brought into service, ran over a mine and went down with its entire crew, but by that time Marinesko had become an officer on another submarine.

From Berne by way of Zurich, and then past various lakes. In his book, Party member Diewerge did not bother with landscape descriptions as he traced the path of the traveling medical student. And the chain-smoker, now in the seventh year of his studies, probably took little notice of the mountain ranges drawing ever nearer and eventually closing in the horizon; at most he may have registered the snow that blanketed houses, trees, and mountainsides, and the change in the light each time the train plunged into a tunnel.

David Frankfurter set out on 31 January 1936. He read the newspaper and smoked. Under the heading "Miscellaneous" he found several items on the activities of Landesgruppenleiter Gustloff. The daily papers, among them the *Neue Zürcher Zeitung* and the *Basler Nationalzeitung,* documented that date, reporting on everything happening at the time or likely to happen in the future. At the beginning of this year, destined to go down in history as the year of the Olympic Games in Berlin, fascist Italy had not yet conquered Abyssinia, the distant kingdom of Haile Selassie, and in Spain war was looming. In the German Reich, construction of the Autobahn was progressing nicely, and in Langfuhr Mother was eight and a half. Two summers earlier her brother Konrad, the deaf-mute with curly locks, had drowned swimming in the Baltic. He was her favorite brother. That explained why, when my son was born forty-six years later, he had to be christened Konrad; but most people call him Konny, and his girlfriend Rosi addresses him in her letters as "Conny."

Diewerge tells us that the Landesgruppenleiter came home on 3 February, tired from a successful trip through the Swiss cantons. Frankfurter knew he would arrive in Davos on the third. In addition to the daily papers, David regularly read *Der Reichsdeutsche,* the Party newsletter Gustloff issued, which listed the dates of all his appearances. David knew almost everything about his chosen target. He had inhaled as many particulars as he could hold. But was he also aware that the previous year the Gustloffs had used their savings to have a solid house built in Schwerin, of glazed brick, even furnished in anticipation of their planned return to the Reich? And that both of them fervently wished for a son?

When the medical student reached Davos, fresh snow had just fallen. The sun was shining, and the resort looked just as it did on postcards. He had set out without luggage, but with his mind made up. From the *Basler Nationalzeitung* he had ripped a photograph of Gustloff in uniform: a tall man with an expression of strained determination and a high forehead, which he owed to his receding hairline.

Frankfurter billeted himself in the Lion. He had to wait until Tuesday, 4 February. In Genesis, on this day of the week the expression "Ki tov," indicating that God saw that the Creation was good, appears twice, for which reason Jews consider Tuesday a lucky day—I picked this up on the Internet. On the home page, by now so familiar, this date was dedicated to the memory of the martyr.

Smoking in the sun on hard-crusted snow. Every step crunched. Monday was spent on seeing the town. Back and forth, back and forth along the main promenade. Watching an ice hockey game, an unobtrusive spectator among other spectators. Casual conversations with visitors to the resort. His breath forming a white cloud. Avoid arousing suspicion! Not a word too many. Nice and easy. Everything was prepared. He had bought a revolver without the slightest difficulty and had practiced at the Ostermundingen shooting range, near Berne—all perfectly legal. Sickly though he was, his hand had proved steady.

On Tuesday, close to his destination a weatherproof sign, WILHELM GUSTLOFF NSDAP, came to his aid: from the main promenade a street called Am Kurpark branched off, leading to house number 3. A watery blue stuccoed building with a flat roof, its gutters garnished with icicles. Few streetlights to hold the gathering darkness at bay. No snow falling.

So much for the scene from outside. Additional details held no significance. How the deed itself unfolded, only the perpetrator and the widow could say later on. I accessed the interior of the portion of the house in question with the help of a photograph inserted beside the indented text on the aforementioned home page. The photo was apparently taken after the crime, for three fresh bouquets of flowers on various tables and a dresser, along with a blooming flowerpot, lend the room the air of a shrine.

When the bell rang, Hedwig Gustloff opened the door. A young man, whose "nice eyes" she mentioned in her testimony, asked to see the Landesgruppenleiter. He was standing in the corridor, speaking on the telephone with Party member Dr. Habermann from the local office in Thun. As he passed him, Frankfurter allegedly heard him saying "Foul Jews," which Frau Gustloff later disputed: she averred that such terms were foreign to her husband, although he did consider the solution of the Jewish Question urgent.

She escorted the visitor into her husband's study and invited him to have a seat. No suspicion. Petitioners often came unannounced, including fellow Nazis in financial difficulties.

As the medical student sat there in his armchair, still in his coat and with his hat on his knees, he could see the desk, on it a clock in a slightly curved wooden case, and on the wall above it the honorary SA dagger. Above and to the side of the dagger hung an assortment of pictures of the Führer/Reich chancellor, room decor in black and white and color. No picture of Gustloff's mentor, Gregor Strasser, murdered two years earlier. To one side a model sailing ship, probably the training vessel *Gorch Fock*.

As he waited, the visitor, who forbade himself to smoke, would also have been able to see the radio on a chest of drawers next to the desk, and beside it a bust of the Führer, in either bronze or plaster painted to look like bronze. The cut flowers on the desk that appear in the photograph may have filled a vase before the deed, lovingly arranged by Frau Gustloff to welcome her husband home after a strenuous journey, also as a belated birthday greeting.

On the desk, odds and ends and loosely stacked papers: perhaps reports from the cantonal Party chapters, doubtless also correspondence with offices in the Reich, probably a few threatening letters, which had been arriving frequently of late; but Gustloff had refused police protection.

He strode into the study without his wife. Straight-backed and robust, having shaken off his tuberculosis years before, he advanced in civilian dress toward his visitor, who did not rise from the armchair but fired from a seated position only seconds after he drew the revolver from his overcoat pocket. Well-aimed shots made four holes in the Landesgruppenleiter's chest, neck, and head. He collapsed, without crying out, under the framed pictures of his Führer. In no time his wife was in the room, first catching sight of the revolver still aimed at its target, then seeing her fallen husband, who, as she bent over him, was bleeding to death from all the wounds.

David Frankfurter, the traveler with a one-way ticket, put on his hat and left the site of his premeditated deed, without being detained by the building's other residents, who by this time had become aware that something was going on. He wandered around in the snow for a while, slipping and falling several times, had the emergency number memorized, named himself as the perpetrator from a telephone booth, eventually located the nearest police station, and turned himself in to the cantonal police.

He made the following confession to the officer on duty and later repeated it in court without changing a word: "I fired the shots because I am a Jew. I am fully aware of what I have done and have no regrets."

After that a great deal appeared in print. What Wolfgang Diewerge characterized as "a cowardly murder" turned in the hands of the novelist Emil Ludwig into "David's struggle with Goliath." These diametrically opposed assessments have survived into the digitally networked present. Before long everything that followed, including the trial, outgrew the perpetrator and his victim and assumed mythic significance. The hero of biblical proportions, who hoped his clear-cut act of defiance would summon his tormented people to resistance, was juxtaposed with the martyr for the National Socialist movement. Both were supposed to find their places in the book of history, figures larger than life. The perpetrator, however, soon sank into obscurity; even Mother, when she was a child and was called Tulla, never heard anything about a murder and a murderer, only fairy tales of a gleaming white ship that took loads of merry folk on long and short cruises for an organization calling itself Strength through Joy.

2

WHILE I WAS STILL A FOOT-DRAGGING STUDENT living off the generosity of others, I attended the lectures given by Professor Höllerer at Berlin's Technical University. He captivated the overflowing crowd in the lecture hall with his piercing birdlike voice. His subject matter was the dramatists Kleist, Grabbe, and Büchner, all geniuses on the run. One of his courses was called Between Classicism and Modernism. I liked hanging out in the Waitzkeller among the young literary types and still younger girls, booksellers' apprentices. Here unpolished literary attempts were read aloud and critiqued. At the Literary Colloquium's branch on Carmerstrasse I even took a course based on the American notion of teaching creative writing. A good dozen promising fellow students, some with actual talent. I didn't have the right stuff, I was told firmly by one of the instructors, who was trying to prod us beginners with topics like Spiritual Help Line into taking epic leaps. The best I could hope to produce was trashy novels. But now he has hauled me out of the pit into which he cast me back then, declaring that my botched life has its origin in a unique event, an exemplary event, an event worthy of being told.

Some of the talents from that era are already dead. Two or three of them made a name for themselves. My old instructor, however, seems to have written himself dry; otherwise he would hardly have pressed me into service as a ghostwriter. But I've had enough of this crab-walk. I keep getting stuck. I tell him it's not worth it. Both of those fellows were nutcases, one no better than the other. Sacrificing himself to give his people an example of heroic resistance—don't make me laugh. The Jews weren't one iota better off after the murder. On the contrary! Terror was the law of the land. And two years later, when the Jew Herszel Grynszpan shot the German diplomat Ernst von Rath in Paris, the Nazis' response was the Night of Broken Glass. And what good did another martyr do the Nazis, I wonder. Well, all right, they named a ship after him.

And already I'm back on track. Not because the old man is breathing down my neck, but because Mother has never eased up. Even when I was a boy in Schwerin, where I had to hop around like a puppet on a string in my blue shirt and neckerchief every time some dedication took place, she would hammer away at me: "That sea there full of ice, and them poor little ones all floating head down. You've got to write about it. That much you owe us, seeing as how you were one of the lucky ones and survived. Someday I'll tell you the whole story, exactly what happened, and you'll write it all down . . ."

But I wasn't willing. No one wanted to hear the story, not here in the West, and certainly not in the East. For decades the *Gustloff* and its awful fate were taboo, on a pan-German basis, so to speak. Yet Mother continued to badger me, now by secret courier. When I dropped out of the university and went to work for Springer, listing fairly far to the right, she saw an opportunity even there: "That man's a revanchist. He sides with us expellees. He'll print it in installments, for however many weeks it takes..."

And later, when the *Tageszeitung* and my various other left-leaning headstands were making me dizzy, Aunt Jenny would invite me to join her for asparagus and new potatoes at Habel's near Roseneck and serve up Mother's admonitions for dessert: "My girlfriend Tulla still places great hopes in you. She wants me to let you know that it's your filial duty to tell the whole world..."

But I didn't let myself be pressured. All those years when I was freelancing, writing long pieces for nature publications, on organic vegetables and the effects of acid rain on Germany's forests, for instance, also breast-beating stuff along the lines of "Auschwitz: Never Again," I managed to leave the circumstances of my birth out of it—until that fateful day at the end of January '96 when I first clicked my way to the right-wing extremist Stormfront home page, and from there followed some Gustloff links until I landed on the www. blutzeuge.de site and made the acquaintance of the Comrades of Schwerin.

Took some initial notes. Was amazed. Wanted to understand how this provincial celebrity, who owed his fame to those four shots in Davos, had all of a sudden begun to attract surfers. The site was skillfully done. Photos of key locales in Schwerin, interspersed with little come-ons: "Would you like to learn more about our martyr? Should we offer his story piece by piece?"

What's all this "we" business? This "comrades" business? I was willing to bet that the creator of the site was flying solo out there in cyberspace. One mind was the dung heap where these seeds were sending up Nazi-brown shoots, and one alone. What this fellow had posted on the Net about Strength through Joy looked attractive, and wasn't even all that idiotic. Snapshots of vacationers smiling on board ship, or cavorting on the beaches of Rügen Island.

Of course Mother didn't really know much about all this. She always referred to Strength through Joy as KDF, for "Kraft durch Freude." As a ten-year-old she had seen bits and pieces in Fox's Movietone News, the newsreel shown at the Langfuhr cinema, among them the maiden voyage of "our KDF boat." And Father and Mother Pokriefke had actually had a chance to take a cruise on the *Gustloff* in the summer of '39, he as a worker and Party member, she as a member of the Nazi Women's League. A little group from Danzig—at that time still a free state—was allowed to participate under a special dispensation for German citizens abroad—in the nick of time, so to speak. The destination in mid-August was the Norwegian fjords, too late in the season for the bonus of midnight sun.

During my childhood, whenever Mother brought up her inevitable Sunday topic of the ship's sinking, she would always emphasize her father's enthusiasm for a Norwegian folk-dancing group in colorful costumes who had performed on the sundeck of the KDF ship. "And my mama just loved that swimming pool, with them colorful pictures all done in tiles—that was where those poor naval auxiliary girls was squeezed in like sardines until that Russki blew the poor young things to bits with his second torpedo..."

But at this point the *Gustloff* hasn't even had its keel laid, let alone been launched. Besides, I have to backtrack, because right after the fatal shots were fired, the judges, prosecutor, and defense attorney in the Swiss canton of Graubünden began to prepare for the trial of David Frankfurter. The proceedings were supposed to take place in Chur. Since the perpetrator had confessed, a speedy trial could be expected. But in Schwerin solemn observances were being organized, on orders from the very highest level, to be staged as soon as the body was brought back, and designed to leave a lasting impression on the memory of the German Volk.

What a scene a few well-aimed shots had set in motion: columns of goose-stepping storm troopers, aisles of honor, color guards, uniformed wreath and torch bearers. To muffled drumbeats, the Wehrmacht marched by at a funereal pace, past sidewalks lined with residents of Schwerin, who were paralyzed by grief or merely craning their necks to see the spectacle.

Before his assassination, this Party member had been largely unknown in his native Mecklenburg, just one regional Gruppenleiter among many in the Nazi organizations abroad; but in death Wilhelm Gustloff was inflated into a figure who seemed to render several speakers helpless as they searched for comparable greatness; all that occurred to them was Horst Wessel, that top martyr who had written and lent his name to a song always played and sung on official occasions—of which there were plenty—right after "Deutschland, Deutschland, über alles": "Raise high the flag..."

In Davos the solemnities took place on a more modest scale. The resort's Protestant church, actually a mere chapel, set certain limitations. In front of the altar, draped with a swastika flag, stood the coffin. On top of it lay the deceased's honorary dagger, armband, and SA cap, arranged in a still life. Some two hundred Party members from all the cantons had gathered. In addition, Swiss citizens, both outside and inside the chapel, were there to express their views. The mountains forming a backdrop.

Portions of the rather simple memorial service held in this resort famous the world over for its TB sanatoria were broadcast to all German radio stations. Announcers called upon the listeners to hold their breath. But in all the commentaries and in all the speeches delivered later in other locations, David Frankfurter's name was not mentioned once. From then on he was referred to only as the "treacherous Jewish murderer." When the opposition tried to force-feed the sickly medical student into a hero, placing him because of his Serbian origins on a pedestal as the "Yugoslav Wilhelm Tell," Swiss patriots objected in outraged stage German, but these attempts also spawned questions about possible backers of the young shooter; soon Jewish organizations came under suspicion of pulling his strings. The world Jewish conspiracy was alleged to have ordered the "cowardly murder."

Meanwhile the special train for the coffin stood waiting in Davos. As it pulled out of the station, church bells clanged. The train took from Sunday morning to Monday evening to complete its journey, making its first stop on German soil in Singen, followed by brief, solemn stops in Stuttgart, Würzburg, Erfurt, Halle, Magdeburg, and Wittenberg, where the local Gauleiters and Party honor guards "presented the last salute" to the corpse in the coffin.

I came across this expression, drawn from the glossary of pretentiousness, on the Internet. On the Web site where contemporary reports were posted in their original wording, salutes were not "given" with the raised right hand, in the manner customary at the time and borrowed from the Italian Fascists; no, on all the railroad platforms and at all the observances, people gathered to "present" the final salute; and for that reason at the site www.blutzeuge.de the dead man was memorialized not only with quotations from the Führer's speech and descriptions of the service in Schwerin's festival hall, but also with the German salute, "presented" from that newest dimension known as cyberspace. Only then could the Comrades of Schwerin move on to mention Beethoven's *Eroica* symphony, struck up by the local orchestra.

Yet a carping voice chimed in to challenge this fatuous nonsense being disseminated to the entire world. A chatter corrected the report in the *Völkischer Beobachter* that a Wehrmacht detachment had saluted the war hero Wilhelm Gustloff; he pointed out that because of his weak lungs the honoree had not qualified to participate in the Great War, to demonstrate his courage at the front, and to earn an Iron Cross, whether first or second class.

He seemed pedantic, this lone adversary disrupting the virtual solemnities. He also pointed out that in his speech Mecklenburg's Gauleiter Hildebrandt had failed to mention the "nationalist-Bolshevist influence" Gregor Strasser had exercised over the martyr. One might have expected that the Gauleiter, a onetime farmhand who had hated the big landowners since childhood and had therefore hoped that after the Führer's seizure of power the gentry's estates would be systematically dismantled, would use the occasion to salvage the murdered Strasser's honor, at least by implication. This was the general tenor of the chatter's kvetching. He had a comeback for everything, which gave rise to wrangling in the chat room.

Back on the Web site, the funeral procession got under way, untroubled by the possible outcome of the debate. The scene was brought to life by pictures. In variable weather it wound its way from the festival hall down Gutenbergstrasse and Wismarsche Strasse, then by way of Totendamm and along Wallstrasse to the cremato-rium. Mounted on a gun carriage, the coffin traversed the distance of four kilometers, passing through an aisle of honor, until it was unloaded, to the roll of drums, for the purpose of incineration, and, after receiving a pas-tor's blessing, was slid down a shaft into the flames. A command rang out, and the flags were dipped on either side of the vanishing coffin. Columns of soldiers stand-ing at attention struck up Uhland's song about the dead comrade and extended their right arms to present the very last salute. The Wehrmacht detachment again fired salvos in honor of a combat veteran who, as has already been brought to light, did not experience trench war-fare, and thus was spared all the shelling, or, as Ernst Jünger dubbed it in his eponymous war diary, the "hail of steel." Ah, if only he had been at Verdun, and had bit the dust in a shell crater when the time was right!

Having grown up in the town of the seven lakes, I know the spot where the urn was later buried in a concrete foundation on the southern shore of Lake Schwerin. On top was placed a four-meter-high piece of granite, whose chiseled cuneiform inscription waxed eloquent. Together with the gravestones of other early members of the movement, it formed the memorial grove around a hall of honor built for the occasion. I don't recall, but I'm sure Mother knows exactly when in the postwar period they cleared away everything that might have reminded the townspeople of the martyr—and not only on orders from the Soviet occupying power. But my networked nemesis insisted that a new monument should be erected in the same location; he persisted in calling Schwerin the "Wilhelm Gustloff city."

All past, gone with the wind! Who still recalls the name of the leader of the German Labor Front? Along with Hitler, those whom people mention nowadays as all-powerful are Goebbels, Göring, Hess. On a television quiz show, if questions came up about Himmler or Eichmann, some contestants might have heard of them, but most would draw a total historical blank, and with a little smirk the perky quizmaster would tally up the loss of so-and-so many thousands in prize money.

But who today, besides my Webmaster, bouncing around in the Net, knows anything about Robert Ley? Yet it was he who dissolved all the labor unions right after the takeover, emptied their coffers, dispatched squads to confiscate everything at their headquarters, and forced all their members, who numbered in the millions, to join the German Labor Front. It was he, this moon face with a cowlick, who had the inspiration to require all state employees, then all teachers and pupils, and finally the workers in all industries to use "Heil Hitler" as their daily greeting. And it was he who came up with the idea of organizing the way workers and white-collar employees spent their holidays. He provided inexpensive trips to the Bavarian Alps and the Erzgebirge, to the North Sea and Baltic coasts, and, last but not least, ocean cruises of shorter or longer duration—all under the motto of "Strength through Joy."

Clearly a man who got things done, for all these mea-
sures were carried out with lightning speed and without
delay, while other things were happening at the same
time and the concentration camps were filling, batch
after batch. Early in '34 Ley chartered the passenger ship
Monte Olivia and the four-thousand-ton steamer *Dresden*
for his planned Strength through Joy fleet. Together
these ships could accommodate just about three thousand passengers. But the *Dresden* was on only its eighth
ocean cruise, intended to put the beauty of the Norwegian fjords on display again, when it encountered an underwater granite ledge in the Karmsund that tore a
thirty-meter gash in the ship's hull, whereupon the *Dresden* began to sink. Although all the passengers were
saved, except for two women who died of heart failure,
the loss of the ship threatened to scuttle the entire
Strength through Joy project.

But Ley would have none of that. A week later he
chartered four more passenger ships and now had at his
disposal a fleet capable of expansion; over the following
year it would handle 135,000 vacationers, most of them
taking five-day cruises to Norway, but soon some could
also book Atlantic journeys to the favored destination of
Madeira. It cost only forty reichsmarks to achieve joy
through strength, plus ten for a special excursion train to
the Hamburg harbor.

As a journalist leafing through the source materials
available to me, I asked myself: How did this state, legit-
imized by a questionable enabling act and the sole political party left in existence, manage within such a short

time to induce all the workers and salaried employees organized into the German Labor Front not only not to protest but even to cooperate, and soon to engage in mass rejoicing on command? Partial credit can go to the activities of the Nazi organization Strength through Joy, about which many survivors of those years continued to rave in private; Mother even did so openly: "Suddenly everything was changing. My papa—he was only a carpenter's helper and didn't really believe in anything anymore—he just couldn't say enough about that KDF ship. See, that was the first chance he ever had in his whole life to go on a trip with my mama..."

Here I should mention that Mother has always had this tendency to speak her mind too loudly and at just the wrong moment. She either rejects things or hangs on to them for dear life. When she heard in March '53 that Stalin had died—I was eight and in bed with tonsillitis, German measles, or measles—she lit candles in our kitchen and cried her eyes out. I never saw her cry that way again. Years later, when Ulbricht was forced off the stage, I heard that she mocked his successor as "that roofer." Although a declared antifascist, she bewailed the destruction in the early '50s of the monument to Wilhelm Gustloff, cursing the "scum" who had desecrated the grave. Later, when we in the West were experiencing terrorism, I gathered from one of her messages smuggled from Schwerin that she believed "Baadermeinhof," whom she pictured as one person, had fallen in the fight against fascism. It remained impossible to tell whose side she would take in any given situation. When Jenny heard about Mother's apodictic statements, she just smiled: "That's always been Tulla's way. She says things other people don't wish to hear. Of course she sometimes exaggerates just a bit..." To give another example, at a meeting of her collective, Mother apparently once declared in front of all her comrades that she was "Stalin's last faithful follower," and in the next breath held up the classless KDF society as the model for every true Communist.

In January '36, the Hamburg shipbuilding company Blohm and Voss was commissioned to build a passenger ship for the German Labor Front and its subsidiary Strength through Joy, a ship slated to cost 25 million reichsmarks; no one asked where all that money was coming from. At first only statistics were available: 25,484 gross metric tons, a length of 208 meters, and a draft of 6 to 7 meters. The top speed was supposed to be 15.5 knots, and the ship was to carry a crew of 417 and 1,463 passengers. Those were normal figures for ships being built at the time, but in contrast to other passenger ships this new one was supposed to erase class distinctions for the present, having only one passenger class, which, according to Robert Ley's directives, was to set an example for the desired unity of the German Volk.

The plan called for naming the new ship after the Führer, but as the Reich chancellor sat next to the widow at the memorial service for the Party comrade murdered in Switzerland, he reached the decision that the KDF ship being built should bear the name of the movement's

most recent martyr; accordingly, soon after Gustloff's
cremation, public squares, streets, and schools were given
his name. Even a plant that manufactured weapons and
other military hardware, the Simson Works in Suhl,
was renamed, after its compulsory Aryanization, so that
the Wilhelm Gustloff Works might serve the cause of
rearmament and, from '42 on, operate a branch in the
Buchenwald concentration camp.

It would take too long to list all the other things
named after him, so I shall mention only the Gustloff
Bridge in Nuremberg and the Gustloff House serving
the German colony in Brazil's Curitiba. Instead I must
ask myself the question, which I also posted on the Internet: "What if the ship whose keel was laid in Hamburg on 4 August 1936 had been named after the Führer
after all?"

The answer came promptly: "The *Adolf Hitler* would
never have sunk, because Providence would have..."
Etc., etc. This reply set the following train of thought in
motion: in that case, I would not have been forced to
skulk around as the survivor of a disaster forgotten by
the whole world. If I had disembarked at Flensburg perfectly normally, and Mother had given birth to me there,
I would not have been an exemplary case, and today
would not provide any cause for quibbling.

"My Paulie's something special!" Mother's standard
phrase rang in my ears throughout my childhood. It was
embarrassing when she rambled on in her broadest
Langfuhr idiom to neighbors and even her Party collec-

tive about my special qualities: "From the time he was born, I just knew this kid was going to be real famous someday..."

Don't make me laugh! I know my limitations. I'm a run-of-the-mill journalist, who can do a decent job for short stretches. I used to have big plans—a book that I never got around to writing was supposed to be called "Between Springer and Dutschke"—but for the most part my plans stayed on the drawing board. Then Gabi stopped taking the Pill without telling me, was soon pregnant, undeniably by me, and dragged me off to City Hall to get married. Once the squalling baby was there and the future educator had gone back to her studies, it was clear as day to me: From now on, don't expect much. The best you can do is hold up your end as a house-husband, changing diapers and vacuuming. No more delusions of grandeur! What can you say about a guy who lets himself be saddled with a baby when he's thirty-five and losing his hair? Love? Forget about that till you're past seventy, and by then the parts will have stopped working anyway.

Gabriele, whom everyone called Gabi, wasn't exactly pretty, but she sure could turn a man on. She was the take-charge type, and in the beginning she thought she could spur me to adopt a more energetic gait—"Why don't you tackle something with social relevance, like the arms buildup and the peace movement?"—and I managed to grind out a preachy piece on Mutlangen, the stationing of Pershing 2 missiles, and the sit-ins, which was well received even in halfway leftist circles. But then the oomph went out of me again. And at some point she must have decided I was a lost cause.

Gabi wasn't the only one; Mother, too, saw me as a typical failure. Right after the birth of our son, and when she had made her wish about his name known by telegram—"Must call him Konrad"—she minced no words in letters to her friend Jenny: "What a fool! For this he went west? To let me down? Is this all he can deliver?"

She was right. My wife, who was ten years my junior, remained ambitious. She passed all her exams, became a secondary-school teacher, got tenure, while I stayed in my rut. The exhausting fun and games lasted not quite seven years; then it was all over between Gabi and me. She left me the apartment in Kreuzberg, with its coal stove and the stultifying atmosphere of that part of Berlin that nothing can dispel, and moved with little Konrad to Mölln in West Germany, where she had family and soon found a teaching job.

A peaceful little town, attractively situated on a lake, with the East German border nearby, to all appearances idyllic. That rather pretty part of Germany styles itself pretentiously "the Duchy of Lauenburg." Like something from a bygone era. In travel guides Mölln is known as the "Eulenspiegel town." And because Gabi had spent her childhood there, in no time she felt right at home.

But I continued to go downhill. Was stuck in Berlin. Kept my head above water doing hackwork for a wire service, writing the occasional feature article on the side—"What's Green about Berlin's International Green Week?" and "Turks in Kreuzberg"—for the *Protestant Sunday Weekly*. Other than that? A couple of relationships, more annoying than anything else, and parking tickets. Oh yes, a year after Gabi left, the divorce went through.

I saw my son Konrad only on visits, which meant not often and at irregular intervals. A boy in glasses who I thought was shooting up too fast, though in his mother's eyes he was doing fabulously in school, was gifted and sensitive. But when the Wall came down in Berlin and the border opened up near Mustin, just past Ratzeburg, the next town over from Mölln, Konny begged my ex to drive him to Schwerin right away—it was a good hour away—to see his Grandma Tulla.

That's what he called her. At her request, I assume. It didn't end with that one visit—unfortunately, I would have to say today. The two of them hit it off at once. Even as a ten-year-old Konny had a fairly precocious way about him. I'm sure Mother got him hooked on her stories, which of course weren't confined to the carpentry shop on Elsenstrasse in Langfuhr. She dredged up everything, including her adventures as a streetcar conductor during the last year of the war. The boy must have soaked it up like a sponge. Of course she also poured on the tale of the endlessly sinking ship. From then on, Konny, or "Konradchen," as Mother called him, was her great hope.

Around this time she often drove to Berlin in her Trabi. She was retired by now, and seemed to have been bitten by the travel bug. But she really came only to see her friend Jenny; I was an afterthought. What a reunion! Whether in Aunt Jenny's doll's house or in my hole-in-the-wall in Kreuzberg, all she could talk about was Konradchen, the joy of her old age. How nice that she had more time to devote to him, now that the People's Own Furniture Combine had been dismantled—with her assistance, by the way. She was glad to help the process along any way she could. Her advice was in demand again. As for her grandson, she had all sorts of plans.

In response to such overabundant energy, Aunt Jenny merely offered her a frozen little smile. Meanwhile I had to listen to remarks such as "My Konradchen's going to be something. Not a failure like you..."

"Right," I told her, "I haven't amounted to much, and it's too late now. But as you see, Mother, I'm developing— if you can call it that—into a chain-smoker."

Like that Jew Frankfurter, I would add today; he, too, lit one cancer stick from the last, and now I really can't help writing about him, because the shots struck their target, and because the building of the ship in Hamburg was moving along nicely, and because a navigator named Marinesko was serving on a seaworthy submarine along the Black Sea coast, and because on 9 December 1936 the trial got under way before the high court of the Swiss canton of Graubünden against the Yugoslav-born murderer of the German citizen Wilhelm Gustloff.

In Chur three guards in plain clothes stood in front of the judges' bench and the dock, where the defendant was flanked by two police officers. On orders from the cantonal police, the guards kept their eyes on the audience as well as on the journalists from home and abroad; some kind of violence was feared, from one quarter or the other.

The large crowd of spectators from the German Reich had made it necessary to relocate the proceedings from the cantonal court to the chamber of the Graubünden parliament. An elderly gentleman with a white goatee, Eugen Curti, was the attorney for the defense. As coplaintiff, the widow of the murdered man was represented by the noted law professor Friedrich Grimm, who would cause quite a stir after the war with a work destined to become a classic—*Political Justice: The Blight of Our Era*. I was not surprised to discover that a new edition of the book was being peddled on the Internet by the German Canadian right-wing extremist Ernst Zündel, but in the meantime this Nazi-inspired work has apparently gone out of print again.

I am fairly certain, however, that my Schwerin Webmaster ordered a copy while it was still available, for his Internet site bristles with Grimm quotations and polemical retorts to the admittedly long-winded defense offered by Curti. It seems as though the case is being retried, this time on a virtual world stage before an overflow crowd of onlookers.

Later my research would reveal that my lone combatant owed some of his inside dope to the *Völkischer Beobachter*. He mentioned in passing, for instance, that when Frau Hedwig Gustloff, dressed in black, entered the courtroom on the second day of the trial, the Germans present, as well as some Swiss sympathizers and the journalists who had come from the Reich, all stood up and greeted her with the Hitler salute; this account was lifted from pages of the "Battle Organ of the National Socialist Movement of Greater Germany." The *VB* had a presence not only during the four days of the undeniably historic trial but also on the Internet; the quotations from the stern father's letter to his prodigal son spread by way of the Net also came straight from that Nazi organ, for the rabbi's letter—"I expect nothing more of you. You do not write. Now it will do no good to write..."— was quoted in court by the prosecution as evidence of the defendant's heartlessness; the court, however, was probably kind enough to allow the chain-smoker a cigarette or two during breaks in the proceedings.

While the submarine officer Marinesko was either out to sea or on shore leave in the Black Sea port of Sebastopol, and presumably spent his three days on land plastered out of his mind, and while the new ship was rapidly taking shape in Hamburg, with riveting hammers setting the tone day and night, the defendant David Frankfurter sat or stood between the two cantonal police officers. He eagerly confessed to the charges. That robbed the trial of any suspense. He sat and listened, then stood up and said: I made up my mind, purchased, practiced, traveled, found, entered, sat down, shot five times. He made these admissions straightforwardly, with only occasional hesitation. He accepted the verdict, but on the Internet he was characterized as "weeping pathetically."

Since capital punishment was not legal in the canton of Graubünden, Professor Grimm regretfully demanded the harshest penalty available: life imprisonment. Up to the announcement of the sentence—eighteen years in the penitentiary, to be followed by deportation—the online account unambiguously favored the martyr, but after that my Webmaster parted company from the Comrades of Schwerin. Or was he no longer alone? Had that caviler and know-it-all returned, the one who had shown up in the chat room once before? At any rate, a kind of quarrelsome role-playing set in.

The dispute that from now on repeatedly flared up was conducted on a first-name basis: a Wilhelm spoke for the murdered Landesgruppenleiter, and a David assumed the part of the would-be suicide.

It was as if this exchange of blows were taking place in the hereafter. Yet the attention to detail was very much of this world. Each time the murderer and the murderee met, the deed and the motivation for it were thoroughly chewed over. While one of the parties spewed propaganda, proclaiming, for instance, that at the time of the trial there were 800,000 fewer unemployed in the Reich than in the previous year, and declaring enthusiastically, "This we owe to the Führer alone," the other party reproachfully enumerated all the Jewish doctors and patients who had been driven out of hospitals and sanatoria, and pointed out that the Nazi regime had called for a boycott of Jews as early as 1 April 1933, whereupon the windows of Jewish shops had been smeared with the hate slogan "Death to the Jews!" Back and forth it went. If Wilhelm posted quotations from the Führer's *Mein Kampf* on his site to support his thesis of the necessity of preserving the purity of the Aryan race and German blood, David replied with passages from *The Moor Soldiers,* a report by a former concentration-camp inmate that a Swiss publishing house had issued.

The battle raged in deadly earnest, with both sides manifesting grim determination. But suddenly the tone lightened, turned chatty in the chat room. When Wilhelm asked, "So why did you fire five shots at me?" David replied, "Sorry, the first shot was a dud. There were only four entry wounds." To which Wilhelm responded, "True. But who provided the revolver?" David: "I bought the Ballermann myself. For a measly ten Swiss francs." "Pretty cheap for a weapon a person would have to shell out at least fifty francs for." "I see what you're driving at. You think someone must have given it to me. Is that it?" "I don't think—I'm positive you didn't act alone." "Well, that's true! I was acting on behalf of Jews everywhere."

This remained the tenor of their Internet dialogue for the next few days. No sooner had they finished each other off than they began bantering back and forth, as if they were friends fooling around. Before they left the chat room, they said, "See you, you cloned Nazi pig," and, "Take care of yourself, Jewboy!" But the moment a surfer from the Balearic Islands or Oslo tried to elbow his way into their conversation, they would turn on him and drive him away: "Beat it!" or "Come back later!"

Apparently both of them played Ping-Pong, for they were great fans of the German champion Jörg Rosskopf, who, David mentioned, had even defeated a Chinese champion. Both declared their allegiance to fair play. And both revealed themselves as history mavens, willing to admire each other for newly uncovered information: "Terrific! Where did you find that Gregor Strasser quote?" or, "That's something I didn't know, David— that Hildebrandt was booted out by the Führer for left-ist deviation, then reinstalled as Gauleiter when the good old Mecklenburgers stuck up for him."

They could have been taken for friends, they went to so much trouble to work off their mutual hatred, like a debt. When Wilhelm lobbed a question into the chatroom—"If the Führer brought me back to life, would you shoot me again?"—David answered promptly, "No, next time you can blow me away."

Something was dawning on me. Already I was letting go of the notion that a lone Webmaster was skillfully engaging in ghostly role-playing. I had fallen into the clutches of two pranksters who were deadly serious.

Later, when all those involved swore they hadn't had a clue and made a big show of being appalled, I said to Mother, "The whole thing seemed odd to me from the beginning. I was wondering why young people today would be fascinated by this Gustloff and everything connected with him. I realized right away that they weren't a couple of old farts frittering away their time on the Internet, I mean has-beens like you..."

Mother didn't answer. As always when something came too close for comfort, she made her I'm-not-home face, rolling her eyes to the point of no return. She was convinced in any case that a thing like this could happen only because for years and years "you couldn't bring up the *Yustloff*. Over here in the East we sure as hell couldn't. And when you in the West talked about the past, it was always about other bad stuff, like Auschwitz and such. Lordy, lordy! You should've seen how they carried on in the Party collective that time I just mentioned something positive about the KDF ships—that the *Yustloff* was a classless ship..."

And that brought to mind her mama and papa, and their trip to Norway: "My mama just couldn't get over it that the passengers all ate in the same dining room, simple workers like my papa, but also government employees and even top brass in the Party. It must've been almost like what we had in the GDR, only even nicer..."

The idea of a classless ship was a real hit. I assume that explains why the dockworkers cheered like crazy when the new ship, eight stories high, was launched on 5 May 1937. The funnel, the bridge, and the compass platform had not yet been added. All of Hamburg came out to watch, countless thousands. But for the christening only ten thousand Party members, personally invited by Ley, could get up close.

Hitler's special train pulled into Dammtor Station at ten in the morning. From there an open Mercedes drove him, saluting with his arm sometimes outstretched, sometimes flexed, through the streets of Hamburg, to wild cheering, of course. From the Landungsbrücken a motor launch carried him to the shipyard. All the ships in the harbor, including the foreign ones, had hoisted flags. And the entire KDF fleet, made up of chartered vessels, from the *Sierra Cordoba* to the *St. Louis,* lay at anchor dressed to the topmast.

I won't bother to list all the formations lined up, all those who clicked their heels in salute. Below the christening platform swarmed the shipyard workers, cheering as he mounted the stairs. At the last free election, only four years earlier, most of them had voted socialist or communist. Now there was just the one and only party left; and here was the Führer in the flesh.

Not until he was on the stand did he encounter the widow. He knew Hedwig Gustloff from the earliest days of the struggle. Before the failed march to the Feldherrenhalle in Munich in '23, which ended in bloodshed, she had served as his secretary. Later, when he was imprisoned in the fortress of Landsberg, she had gone looking for work in Switzerland and found her husband.

Who else was allowed on the platform? The manager of the shipyard, Staatsrat Blohm, and the head of the works organization, a man called Pauly. Of course Robert Ley stood next to him. But other Party bigwigs as well. Gauleiter Kaufmann of Hamburg and Gauleiter Hildebrandt of Schwerin-Mecklenburg also had permission to be there. The navy was represented by Admiral Raeder. And the local Gruppenleiter of the NSDAP in Davos, Böhme, had not hesitated to undertake the long journey.

Speeches were delivered. This time he held back. After Kaufmann, the manager of the Blohm and Voss shipyard spoke: "To you, my Führer, I report in the name of the shipyard: This cruise ship, production number 511, is ready for launching!"

Everything else deleted. But perhaps I should pick a few plums out of Robert Ley's christening address. The fancy-free salutation was "My fellow Germans!" And then he ventured far afield to celebrate Strength through Joy, his plan for the well-being of the Volk, finally revealing its originator: "The Führer gave me this order: 'See to it that the German worker gets his holidays, that his nerves may remain sound, for do what I might, it would all be for naught if the German people did not have its nerves in order. What matters is that the German masses, the German worker, be strong enough to grasp my ideas.'"

When the widow performed the christening a bit later with the words "I christen you with the name Wilhelm Gustloff," the cheering of the strong-nerved masses drowned out the sound of the champagne bottle being smashed against the bow of the ship. Both the Horst Wessel and the Deutschland songs were sung as the new vessel glided down the slipway... But whenever I, the survivor of the *Gustloff,* attend a launching as a reporter or see one on television, an image steals into the picture: that ship, christened and launched in the most beautiful May weather, sinking in the icy Baltic.

At about this time, when David Frankfurter was already locked up in Chur's Sennhof Prison, and in Hamburg the champagne bottle was smashed on the bow, Aleksandr Marinesko was in either Leningrad or Kronstadt, participating in a training course for naval commanders. At any rate, he had been ordered transferred from the Black Sea to the eastern end of the Baltic. That summer, while the purge trials set in motion by Stalin were not sparing the admiralty of the Baltic fleet, he became commander of a submarine.

M-96 belonged to an older class of boats, suitable for reconnoitering and combat in coastal waters. In the information available to me, I read that *M-96,* with 250 tons of displacement and a length of forty-five meters, was on the small side, carrying a crew of eighteen. For a long time Marinesko remained the commander of this naval unit equipped with only two torpedo tubes, whose range extended as far as the Gulf of Finland. I assume that along the coast he repeatedly practiced surface attacks followed by rapid submerging.

3

WHILE THE INTERIOR, FROM THE LOWEST DECK, the E deck, to the sundeck was being done, the funnel, the bridge, and the communications station were being added, and along the Baltic coast diving practice was taking place, in Chur eleven months of incarceration passed. Only then could the ship leave the fitting-out quay and sail down the Elbe for its trial run in the North Sea. So I will pause until enough seconds have elapsed in the present to allow my narrative to start rolling again. Or should I in the meantime risk a quarrel with someone whose grumbling can't be ignored?

He is calling for distinct memories. He wants to know how Mother looked, smelled, felt to me when I was about three. He says, "First impressions determine the course of a person's life." I say, "What's there to remember? When I was three, she'd just finished her apprenticeship in carpentry. Well, all right, shavings and blocks that she brought home from the shop—I can see them before me in curls and tumbling stacks. I played with shavings and blocks. And what else? Mother smelled of carpenter's glue. Wherever she stood, sat, lay—Lord, yes, her bed!—that smell clung. But because they didn't have child-care centers yet, she left me with a neighbor at first, then in a nursery school. That's what all working mothers did in the Workers' and Peasants' State, not only in Schwerin. I can remember women, fat and skinny, who ordered us around, and semolina pudding so thick your spoon would stand up in it."

But memory scraps like these don't satisfy the old man. He refuses to let me off the hook: "When she was ten, Tulla Pokriefke had a face with two periods for eyes, a comma for a nose, and a dash for a mouth; but what did she look like as a young woman and journeyman carpenter, around 1950, let's say, when she was twenty-three? Did she wear makeup? Did she put a kerchief over her head, or wear one of those matronly flowerpot hats? Was her hair straight, or did she get it permed? Did she ever run around in curlers on the weekend?"

I don't know whether the information I can offer will shut him up; my image of Mother when she was young is both sharp and blurry. I never saw her with anything but white hair. She had white hair from the beginning. Not silvery white, just white. Anyone who asked Mother about it would receive the following explanation: "It happened when my son was born. That was on the torpedo boat that rescued us…" And anyone willing to hear more would learn that from that moment on she had snow-white hair, also in Kolberg, when the survivors, mother and infant, went ashore from the torpedo boat *Löwe*. In those days she wore her hair chin-length.

But earlier, before she turned white "as if on command from way up there," her hair had been naturally almost blond, with a reddish tinge, falling to her shoulders.

In response to further questions—he won't let go—I assure my employer that we have very few photos of my mother from the fifties. One of them shows her wearing her white hair cropped short, matchstick length. It crackled when I ran my hand over it, which she sometimes allowed me do. And as an old woman she still wears it that way. She had just turned seventeen when she turned white from one moment to the next. "Of course not! Mother never dyed her hair, or had it dyed. None of her comrades ever saw her with raven locks or Titian-red ones."

"And what else? What other memories are there? Men, for example: were there any?" He means men who spent the night. As a teenager, Mother was boy crazy. Swimming at Brösen's public bathing area or serving as a streetcar conductor on the Danzig-Langfuhr-Oliva line, she always had boys swarming around her, but also grown men—for instance, soldiers on furlough. "Did she get over men later, when she was white-haired and a mature woman?"

What does the old man think? Maybe he really pictures Mother living like a nun, simply because the shock had bleached her hair. No, there were more than enough men. But they didn't stick around very long. One of them was a foreman bricklayer and very nice. He brought us things that were hard to come by, even if you had ration stamps: liverwurst, for example. I was already ten when he would sit in the kitchen of our rear-courtyard shack at 7 Lehmstrasse and snap his suspenders. His name was Jochen, and he insisted that I ride on his knees. Mother called him "Jochen Two," because in her teens she had known an upper-schooler whose name was Joachim but who went by Jochen. "But that one wasn't interested in me. Wouldn't even touch me..."

At some point Mother must have sent Jochen Two packing, why, I don't know. And when I was about thirteen, a guy from the People's Police would come by after his shift, and sometimes on Sundays too. He was a second lieutenant from Saxony—Pirna, I think. He brought Western toothpaste—Colgate—and other confiscated goods. His name was also Jochen, by the way, for which reason Mother would say, "Number three's coming by tomorrow. Try to be nice to him when he comes..." Jochen Three was sent packing, too, because, as Mother said, he was "bound and determined to marry" her.

She didn't care for marriage. "You're enough of a handful for me," she said, when at fifteen I was fed up with everything. Not with school. There I did fine, except in Russian. But I was fed up with the Free German Youth puppet theater, the harvest deployments, the special operations weeks, the everlasting songs about building socialism, and with Mother too. Just couldn't take it anymore when, usually at Sunday dinner, she would dish up her stories of the *Gustloff* along with the dumplings and mashed potatoes: "Everything started to slither. A thing like that you never forget. It never leaves you. It's not just in my dreams, that cry that spread over the water at the end there. And all them little children among the ice floes..."

Sometimes when Mother sat at the kitchen table after Sunday dinner with her mug of coffee, she would say only, "That sure was one beautiful ship," and then not another word. But her I'm-not-home look spoke volumes.

She was probably right. Once the *Wilhelm Gustloff* was built, and set off on its maiden voyage, gleaming white from stem to stern, by all accounts it was a floating sensation. This opinion was expressed even by people who after the war made much of their having been fervent antifascists from the beginning. And the story went that those privileged to sail on the boat seemed transfigured when they stepped back onto dry land.

For the two-day test run, which happened to take place in stormy weather, they filled the ship with workers and salaried employees from Blohm and Voss, as well as with salesgirls from the Hamburg grocery cooperative. But when the *Gustloff* put out to sea for three days on 24 March 1938, the passengers included a good thousand Austrians, carefully screened by the Party; for two weeks later the people of the Ostmark were supposed to vote in a plebiscite on something that the Wehrmacht had already made a fait accompli with a swift march into that country: the annexation of Austria. On the same voyage three hundred girls from Hamburg came aboard—selected members of the League of German Girls—and well over a hundred journalists.

Just for fun, and as a sort of test, I am now going to

try to picture how your humble servant would have reacted as a journalist to the reception for members of the
press, scheduled for the very beginning of the voyage
and held in the reception-and-movie lounge. As Mother
says, and as Gabi will be happy to tell you, I am anything
but a hero, but perhaps I would have been rash enough
to ask about the financing of the new vessel, and about
the holdings of the German Labor Front, for like the
other journalists I would have been aware that Ley, the
man of many promises, could never have taken on such
ambitious projects without the funds he had skimmed
from all the banned labor unions.

A belated test of courage! If I know myself, the most
I would have come out with is a roundabout query about
the remaining capital, to which the unflappable KDF
tour leader would have promptly responded that the
German Labor Front was swimming in money, as we
could plainly see. In a few days the Howaldt Shipyard
would be launching a huge electrically powered ship,
which, as could already be guessed, would bear the
name of Robert Ley.

After that, the horde of invited journalists had an opportunity to tour the ship. Further questions had to be
swallowed. And as a backdated journalist, I, who in my
entire career have never uncovered a scandal, never de-
tected a skeleton in a closet or misappropriation of campaign funds or bribery of high officials, would have kept
my mouth shut like all the rest. We were permitted only
to express breathless admiration as we made our way
from deck to deck. Except for the special staterooms for

Hitler and Ley, which were not open for inspection, the ship was set up to be purely classless. Although I am acquainted with the details only from photographs and surviving documents, it feels as though I was actually there, impressed and at the same time sweating bullets out of sheer cowardice.

I saw the spacious sundeck, free of irritating superstructures, saw shower stalls and sanitary installations. I saw and assiduously took notes. Later we had a chance to admire the gleaming varnished walls on the lower promenade deck and the nutwood paneling in the lounges. Our mouths open with astonishment, we looked at the Ballroom, the Folk Costume Lounge, the German Hall, and the Music Salon. In all these spaces hung portraits of the Führer, who gazed over our heads, his eyes fixed solemnly but resolutely on the future. In some rooms smaller pictures of Robert Ley were allowed to draw the eye. But the predominant wall decoration consisted of landscapes, oil paintings in old-master style. We inquired about the names of the contemporary artists and noted them on our pads.

In between we were invited to enjoy a draft beer, and I learned to avoid the decadent term "bar," later writing in traditional German terms about the "seven inviting taprooms" on board the KDF ship.

Then they showered us with statistics. In the galley area on A deck, with the help of a supermodern dishwashing setup, 35,000 dirty dishes a day could be rendered spotless. We learned that for every voyage 3,400 metric tons of potable water were on hand, with a tank inside the one funnel serving as the waterworks. When we visited the E deck, where the German League girls from Hamburg had settled into the "swimming youth hostel" with its bunks, we saw on the same deck the indoor swimming pool, with a capacity of sixty metric tons of water. And further numbers, which I did not bother to take down. Some of us were relieved that they spared us the number of tiles and the number of individual chips in a colorful wall mosaic populated by virgins with fish tails and fabulous sea creatures.

Because I have known, ever since the childhood my mother imposed on me, that the second torpedo struck the swimming pool and transformed its tiles and pieces of mosaic into deadly missiles, I might have thought to ask, as I viewed the pool where an energetic swarm of German girls was frolicking, how far below the waterline the pool lay. And on the top deck the twenty-two lifeboats might have struck me as insufficient. But I did not probe, did not invoke the possibility of a catastrophe, did not foresee what would happen seven years later on a bitter-cold night, when the ship was packed—not with a mere fifteen hundred souls, free of their daily cares, as in peacetime, but with close to ten thousand, who sensed their possible doom, and then experienced it in numbers that can only be estimated. Instead I struck up, in shrill or coolly modulated tones, whether as a reporter for the *Völkischer Beobachter* or a correspondent for the solid *Frankfurter Zeitung,* a hymn to the ship's charming lifeboats, as if they were a generous gift from the Strength through Joy organization.

But not long afterward one of the boats had to be lowered into the water. And after that another. And this was no test.

On its second cruise, which took it to the Straits of Dover, the *Gustloff* ran into a nor'wester, and as it was steaming along, full speed ahead, through heavy seas, it picked up an SOS from the English coal boat *Pegaway,* whose cargo hatch had been smashed and its rudder broken. Captain Lübbe, who would die of a heart attack at the beginning of the next Strength through Joy cruise, destination Madeira, immediately set course for the ship in distress. Two hours later, the *Gustloff*'s searchlights picked the *Pegaway* out of the darkness. It was already low in the water. Not until early morning did they manage to lower one of the twenty-two lifeboats, in the face of the worsening storm. But a riptide hurled the lifeboat against the side of the ship, and it drifted off, heavily damaged. Captain Lübbe at once had a motor launch lowered, which after several attempts managed to take aboard nineteen seamen and bring them to safety as the storm subsided. Finally the lifeboat that had drifted off was sighted, and its crew could be rescued.

This incident has been written up. Domestic and foreign papers lauded the heroic rescue. But the only person to provide a thorough account, and at a temporal distance, was Heinz Schön. As I am doing now, he combed through a welter of contemporary news reports. Like mine, his course in life remained tethered to that ill-starred ship. Barely a year before the end of the war, he came on board the *Gustloff* as assistant to the purser. Having risen through the ranks of the Naval Hitler Youth, Schön was hoping to join the navy, but because of poor eyesight was forced to sign on with the merchant marine. After he survived the sinking of the onetime Strength through Joy ship, later hospital ship, still later floating barracks, and eventually refugee transport, he began, when the war was over, to collect and write about everything connected with the *Gustloff,* in good times and bad. This was his sole topic, or the only topic that gripped him.

No doubt Mother would have been very pleased with Heinz Schön's work. But although his books found a publisher in the West, in the GDR they were not welcome. Those who had read his accounts kept mum. On both sides of the German border, in fact, Schön's information was not in demand. Even when a film was made at the end of the fifties—*Night Fell over Gotenhafen*—for which Schön served as an adviser, it achieved only a modest echo. Not long ago a documentary was shown on television, but it still seems as though nothing can top the *Titanic,* as if the *Wilhelm Gustloff* had never existed, as if there were no room for another maritime disaster, as if only the victims of the *Titanic* could be remembered, not those of the *Gustloff.*

But I, too, kept mum, held back, left myself out of the picture, had to be pressured into action. And if I, a fellow survivor, now feel a certain kinship with Heinz Schön, it is only because I can benefit from his obsession. He made lists of everything: the number of cabins, the vast stores of food, the size of the sundeck in square meters, the number of lifeboats, those fully equipped and those missing at the end, and finally, growing from edition to edition, the tally of the dead and the survivors. For a long time his avid collecting took place in obscurity, but now Schön, who is a year older than Mother and whom I could picture as the father of my dreams, which would let me off the hook, is quoted more and more often on the Internet.

Recently the Internet was abuzz with a tearjerker of colossal proportions, the sinking of the *Titanic* freshly filmed in Hollywood and soon to be marketed as the greatest maritime catastrophe of all times. The numbers Schön had soberly cited refuted this nonsense. And this time there *was* an echo, for since the *Gustloff* was launched into cyberspace, making virtual waves, the right-wing scene has been vocal online. Jew bashing is in season again. As if the murder in Davos had taken place just yesterday, radicals are demanding on their Web site "Revenge for Wilhelm Gustloff!" The worst ranting and raving comes from the U.S. and Canada by way of the site associated with a man named Zündel, whose very name suggests something incendiary. But German-language home pages are also springing up, giving free rein to their hate at sites with names such as "National-resistance" and "Thulenet."

Among the first sites to join the debate, if less radical than the others, was www.blutzeuge.de. With the discovery of a ship that not only sank but also, because the whole story was repressed, became the stuff of legend, it was attracting thousands of hits, and more every day. It was to his worldwide web of readers that my lone combatant, who in the meantime had acquired an adversary and fellow sports fan using the screen handle "David," announced with somewhat childish pride the *Gustloff*'s rescue of the shipwrecked English sailors. As if the newspaper accounts were hot off the press, he quoted as a breaking story the British press's praise for this German deed. Then he wanted to know from his antagonist whether the Jewish murderer Frankfurter, imprisoned in Chur, had heard the news. David retorted, "In Sennhof Prison the inmates spent their days at rattling looms and had little time for reading the papers."

Actually David might have found it worthwhile to learn whether a submarine officer called Marinesko, cruising in Baltic coastal waters, had heard about the rescue of the *Pegaway*'s crew by the sailors on the *Gustloff*, and had thus had spelled out for him the name of his predestined target for the first time. But this question did not arise. Instead Webmaster Wilhelm celebrated an event that occurred a short time later: the deployment of the Strength through Joy ship off the English coast as a "floating polling station." Again Wilhelm showed such up-to-date enthusiasm that you would have thought this propaganda coup had been pulled off only recently, not almost sixty years earlier.

At issue was the plebiscite that followed the annexation of Austria to what was now the Greater German Reich. German and Austrian citizens living in England were to be given an opportunity to cast their votes. The voters embarked at the Tilbury docks, and the voting took place outside the three-mile limit. This event occasioned a debate between Wilhelm and David. Back and forth, Ping-Pong-style, went their playful argument about the election. Wilhelm insisted that a secret ballot was ensured by the presence of voting booths; David replied disdainfully that of the almost two thousand voters, a total of four had voted against the Anschluss: "We've seen this before, these 99.9% yes-votes!" Quoting the *Daily Telegraph* of 12 April 1938, Wilhelm countered, "No pressure was exerted! And that, my dear David, was affirmed by Englishmen, who never miss an chance to portray us Germans in a bad light..."

I found the absurd chat-room bickering amusing. But then one of Wilhelm's rejoinders made me smell a rat. This sounded familiar! To blunt David's mockery, he had the temerity to say: "Those democratic elections you glorify are driven by the interests of the plutocrats, of world Jewry! The whole thing is a swindle!"

Something very similar had been offered up recently by my own son. On a visit I had tried to start a conversation by mentioning, with paternal casualness, the story I was doing on the upcoming elections in Schleswig-Holstein; the response I got was, "The whole thing's a swindle. Whether on Wall Street or here: the plutocracy drives everything; money rules."

After the first cruise to Madeira, during which Captain Lübbe died, so that in Lisbon Captain Petersen had to take over for the rest of the voyage, the summer trips to

Norway began, with Captain Heinrich Bertram now in command. There were eleven of these cruises in all, each lasting five days, and so popular that they quickly sold out. They were also on the Strength through Joy schedule the following year. And it was for one of these last cruises to the fjords—I assume the next-to-last one, in mid-August—that Mother's parents were on board.

The local Party headquarters in Langfuhr had actually picked the master carpenter Liebenau and his wife for a trip to Norway because the master owned a German shepherd named Harras, and in the kennels of the Free State's constabulary this Harras had succeeded in covering a bitch whose litter included the Führer's favorite dog, Prinz, a gift to Hitler from the Gauleiter. For this reason the canine sire Harras was mentioned several times in the *Danziger Vorposten*. Mother had sung me this tale since my childhood: her novel-length dog story, complete with pedigree. Any reference to the dog brought the child Tulla into the picture. For instance, when Mother was seven and her brother Konrad drowned while swimming in the Baltic, she supposedly spent a week in the dog kennel in the courtyard of the carpentry shop, during which time she spoke not a word. "I even ate out of his tin bowl. Entrails! You know, the stuff dogs are fed. That was my week in the doghouse, where I didn't say one blessed word, that's how awful I was feeling about our Konrad. He was deaf and dumb from birth, you know..."

But when the dog owner Liebenau, whose son Harry was Mother's cousin, received the offer of a trip to

Norway on the universally beloved Strength through Joy ship, he regretfully turned it down, because his carpentry business was booming: expansion of the barracks out near the airport. He suggested to the Party Kreisleiter that his hardworking helper August Pokriefke, an assiduous Party member, be sent in his stead, along with his wife Erna Pokriefke. Liebenau would cover the cost of their cabin and the already discounted round-trip tickets to Hamburg, using company funds.

"If we still had the photos they snapped on the *Yustloff,* I could show you all the stuff they saw in those few days..." Tulla's mother declared herself particularly taken with the Folk Costume Lounge, the Winter Garden, the morning sing-alongs, and the onboard band that played every evening. Unfortunately the passengers were not allowed to go ashore from the fjords, possibly because of regulations designed to prevent any hard foreign currency from leaving the Reich. But one of the photos, lost along with the album and all the other snapshots, "when the end came for the ship," showed a laughing August Pokriefke dancing with a group of costumed Norwegian folk dancers who had been allowed on board. "My papa, who was basically always full of fun, raved about that ship night and day after he got back from Norway. He supported the Party two hundred percent. That's why he wanted me to join the German Girls League. But I didn't want to. Not then and not later, either, when we was brought back home into the Reich, and all the girls had to be in the BDM..."

Mother's version was probably accurate. She wasn't

one to let others organize her life. Whatever she did had to be voluntary. But even as a member of the Socialist Unity Party and the fairly successful leader of a carpentry brigade that produced bedroom furniture by the ton for the Russians and later usually exceeded its quota during the interior work on the concrete-slab apartment complex in the suburb of Grosser Dreesch, she got herself into hot water by charging that she was surrounded by revisionists and other enemies of the working class. Yet she was also not happy that I had chosen to join the Free German Youth: "Ain't it enough that I'm out here breaking my back for them no-goods?"

My son seems to have a lot in common with Mother. It must be in the genes, as my ex-wife claims. At any rate, Konny never wanted to join anything, not even the Ratzeburg Rowing Club or—Gabi's suggestion—the Boy Scouts. To me she complained, "He's your typical loner, averse to socialization. Some of my colleagues at school say Konny's fixated on the past, no matter how much interest he appears to take in technological progress—computers and modern forms of communication, for instance..."

Yes, of course! It was Mother who gave my son a Mac with all the bells and whistles, not long after the survivors' reunion in Damp, the Baltic coastal resort. He was barely fifteen when she got him hooked. It's her fault and hers alone that things went so wrong with the boy. At least Gabi and I agree on this much: the whole business began when Konny was given that computer.

———

I've never felt comfortable with people who stare at one spot until it smolders, smokes, bursts into flame. Gustloff, for example, whose Führer's will was his command, or Marinesko, who in peacetime practiced only one thing—sinking ships—or David Frankfurter, who in actuality wanted to shoot himself, but then riddled someone else's flesh with four shots to give his people a sign.

In the late sixties the director Rolf Lyssy made a film that had as its subject this man of the sorrowful countenance. I've played the video at home; the black-and-white original has been gone from the theaters for years. Lyssy presents the facts quite accurately. We see the medical student, initially wearing a beret, later a hat, smoking despairingly and downing pills. When he buys the revolver in Berne's Old Town, two dozen bullets cost him three francs seventy. Unlike my version, even before Gustloff enters his study in street clothes, Frankfurter puts on his hat, moves from the armchair to a straight chair, then fires with his hat on. After turning himself in at the Davos police station and reeling off his confession emotionlessly, like a memorized poem recited in school, he places the revolver on the counter as proof.

The film does not tell us anything new. But it has an interesting feature: clips from newsreels that show the coffin, draped in a swastika flag, moving slowly through falling snow. All of Schwerin is snowed in when the funeral procession gets under way. Contrary to the actual reports, only a few civilians salute the coffin with raised right arms. At the trial, the actor playing Frankfurter looks fairly small, standing between two cantonal policemen. He says, "Gustloff was the only one I could get at..." He says, "My intention was to strike the bacillus, not the person..."

The film also shows the prisoner Frankfurter working day after day at a loom, surrounded by other prisoners. Time passes. It becomes clear that during his first years in Chur's Sennhof Prison he gradually recovers from his bone disease; we see him well nourished, plump-cheeked and no longer smoking. Meanwhile, and as if in another film, in the waters along the Baltic coast the submarine commander Aleksandr Marinesko practices rapid diving after an above-water attack, and the Strength through Joy ship *Wilhelm Gustloff* sets out on cruise after cruise to Norway's fjords and the midnight sun.

Of course Lyssy's film shows neither the *Gustloff* nor the Soviet U-boat; only several shots of the looms allow us to surmise from their pounding that as the simple fabric grows, time is passing. And repeatedly the prison doctor certifies to the prisoner Frankfurter that his continuing residence in jail is making him well. It may look as though the perpetrator has already paid for his deed and become a different person, but I still feel uncomfortable with anyone who has one thing, and one only, on his mind—my son, for instance...

She's the one who infected him. For that, Mother, and also for giving birth to me as the ship was sinking, I hate you. I keep having these episodes of hating the simple fact that I survived, for if you, Mother, had gone overboard like thousands of others when the watchword was

"Every man for himself," and in spite of the life jacket over your bulging belly, if you had frozen in the frigid water or been dragged under, together with your unborn, as the ship sank, bow first...

But no. I cannot, must not come to the tipping point of my own accidental existence yet, for the ship still has peaceful Strength through Joy cruises ahead of it. Ten times it rounded the toe of the Italian boot, including Sicily, with shore excursions in Naples and Palermo, because Italy, organized in exemplary fascist fashion, was a friendly nation; here as there the raised right arm was the compulsory salute.

After an overnight train trip, the passengers, always carefully selected, would embark in Genoa. And at the end of the cruise, they would head home by train from Venice. With increasing frequency, high-muckety-mucks from the Party and industry came along, which caused the Strength through Joy ship's classless society to list somewhat. For example, during one cruise the famous inventor of the Volkswagen, originally called KDF-Wagen, was among the guests; Professor Porsche took a particular interest in the ship's state-of-the-art engines.

After wintering in Genoa, the *Gustloff* reached Hamburg again in mid-March of '39. When the *Robert Ley* came into service a few days later, the KDF fleet comprised thirteen ships, but for now the pleasure trips for workers and white-collar employees were over. Seven ships from the fleet, among them the *Ley* and the *Gustloff,* set off down the Elbe for an unannounced destination, and without passengers. Not until they reached

Brunsbüttelkoog were the previously sealed orders opened and the destination revealed: the Spanish port of Vigo.

For the first time the ships were to serve as troop transports. Now that the Civil War was over and General Franco and the Falange had won, the German volunteers of the Condor Legion, fighting at Franco's side since '36, could come home.

Not surprisingly, the military unit that went by this name provided ample fodder for the ever-voracious Internet. Getting a jump on all the others, www.blutzeuge.de reported the return of the Luftwaffe's 88th Flak Regiment. The account of the legionnaires heading for home on the *Gustloff* read as vividly as if they had beaten the Reds only yesterday. My Webmaster delivered his report as a solo; the chat room remained closed, permitting no duet—Wilhelm vs. David—on the subject of the bombardment of Guernica, in the Basque region, by our Junker and Heinkel planes, although these types, whether diving or dropping bombs from a higher altitude, richly illustrated the Web site devoted to the victory celebration.

Initially the spokesman for the Comrades of Schwerin presented himself as a detached expert in military history, indicating that the Spanish Civil War had provided an opportunity for trying out new weaponry, just as the Gulf War had given the Americans a chance a few years back to test their new missile systems. But before long the tone in which he spoke of the Condor Legion became positively lyrical. Apparently he had drawn on

Heinz Schön's painstakingly researched book, for he echoed Schön's enthusiastic description of the ship's return to port and the reception its passengers received. And like the chronicler of the *Gustloff,* whom he repeatedly quoted online, he assumed the role of eyewitness— "Those on board were rejoicing in their smashing success..."—and he reported "deafening applause" when the legionnaires were greeted later by Field Marshal Göring. On the Web site he even posted the musical notation, with all the requisite oom-pah-pah, of the Prussian Grenadiers' March, which the band struck up as the *Gustloff* and the *Ley* tied up at the pier in Hamburg.

While the *Gustloff* was being used as a troop transport for the first time, and David Frankfurter, enjoying much improved health, was serving the third year of his sentence in Sennhof Prison, Aleksandr Marinesko continued undeterred with his practice runs in coastal waters. In the naval archives of the Baltic Red Banner Fleet, a file on the submarine *M-96* has turned up, revealing how successfully the commander drilled his crew for above-water attacks: eventually they were able to submerge a vessel in the record time of 19.5 seconds, as compared to a fleet average of 28 seconds. *M-96* was tested for the real thing. And on the Comrades of Schwerin Web site, too, it looked as if the oft-repeated line from the song "Revenge will come our way one day..." had helped them get ready, if not yet tested, for something undefined— the day of reckoning?

Somehow I could not dismiss the thought that this

person incessantly stirring the Nazi pot and hailing the triumph of the Thousand-Year Reich like a cracked record was not some has-been like Mother but a young man—perhaps a skinhead of the more intelligent sort, or an obsessed schoolboy, engaging in sophistry over the Net. But I did not follow up on my hunch, did not want to admit that certain phrases in these digital postings, such as the seemingly innocuous judgment that "the *Gustloff* was a beautiful ship," had an alarmingly familiar ring. That was not Mother's actual voice, but still...

What I could not shake was the conviction, ticking away like a time bomb, even though I repeatedly tried to bury it, that it could be, no, it *was* my son, who for months now... it was Konrad, who... Behind this lurked Konny...

For a long time I cloaked my hunch in questions: It couldn't possibly be your own flesh and blood, could it? How could a child who was raised in a more or less liberal setting veer so far to the right? Gabi would have noticed—wouldn't she?

But then the Webmaster, who I still hoped was a complete stranger, launched into a tale that was all too familiar: "Once upon a time there was a boy. And he was deaf and dumb, and he drowned while swimming. But his sister, who loved him with all her heart, and who later, much later, would seek safety from the terrors of war by boarding a great ship, did not drown, even when the ship full of refugees was hit by three enemy torpedoes and sank in the frigid waters..."

I felt hot all over: It's him! That's my son telling the

world fairy tales on his Web site, illustrated with comical stick figures. He's revealing family secrets, too, head-on: "But Konrad's sister, who screamed for three days straight after the death of her curly-headed brother, then said not a word for a week, is my beloved grandmother, to whom I have sworn, by the white hair on her head and in the name of the Comrades of Schwerin, that I will testify to the truth, and nothing but the truth: It is the world Jewish conspiracy that aims to pillory us Germans for all eternity..."

And so on and so forth. When I phoned Mother, she showered me with reproaches: "You're a fine one to talk. For years you don't give a shit about our Konradchen, and now all of a sudden you get a bee in your bonnet and start playing the concerned father..."

I also phoned Gabi, and then on the weekend drove to sleepy little Mölln, even bringing flowers. Konny, I heard, was in Schwerin, visiting his grandmother. When I began to unload my worries on my ex, she cut me off: "How dare you come to my house and accuse my son of consorting with right-wing extremists..."

I tried to stay calm, reminding her that only three and a half years ago the idyllic town of Mölln had experienced a terrible fire: two apartment houses where Turks were living had been torched. All the papers had been panting to cover it. Even yours truly had concocted reports for the wire services. Alarm bells had gone off abroad, because it seemed to be starting up again in Germany... There had been three casualties, after all. Several kids were caught, and two were hit with long jail sentences, but perhaps a successor organization, some of these rabid skins, had sought out our Konny. Here in Mölln, or possibly in Schwerin...

She laughed in my face: "Can you picture Konrad with those loudmouths? Be serious! A loner like him in a pack? That's ridiculous. But accusations like yours are typical of the kind of journalism you've always engaged in, no matter who you happened to be working for."

Gabi could not resist reminding me in detail of the time I wrote for the Springer conglomerate, even though thirty years had passed since then. She recalled my "paranoid ravings against leftists": "And by the way, if anyone has secret leanings to the right, it's you; you haven't changed..."

I suppose. I know my own abysses, know how hard it is to keep the lid on. Do my best to remain noncommittal. Generally present myself as neutral. When I have an assignment, regardless of who gave it, I just establish the facts, report what I find, but don't back down...

So because I wanted to find out what was going on—and from Konny himself—I settled into a room not far from my ex, in a hotel overlooking the lake. I kept phoning Gabi, asking to speak with my son. On Sunday evening he finally turned up, having come from Schwerin by bus. At least he wasn't wearing combat boots, only normal suede ankle boots, with jeans and a colorful Norwegian sweater. He actually looked nice, and hadn't shaved off his naturally curly hair. His glasses gave him a know-it-all appearance. He paid no attention to me, had little to say altogether, only a few words to his mother. For supper she served salad and openfaced sandwiches, with apple juice.

But before Konny could disappear into his room after we'd eaten, I waylaid him in the hall. I kept my questions casual: how things were going in school, whether he had friends, maybe a girlfriend, what sports he played, how he liked the birthday present his grandmother had given him—I could guess how much it cost—whether the modern means of communication, like the Internet, for instance, opened up new areas of knowledge for him, what sort of thing he found particularly interesting—if he was into surfing the Net.

He seemed to be listening as I ran through my litany. I thought I could detect a faint smile on his noticeably small mouth. Yes, he was smiling! Then he took off his glasses, put them on again, and looked straight through me, just as he had at the supper table. He answered softly, "Since when do you care what I'm up to?" After a pause—my son was already standing in the doorway to his room—he delivered the knockout punch: "I'm doing historical research. Does that answer your question?"

The door was closed now. I should have called out, "Me too, Konny, me too!" The same old stories. It's about a ship. In May '39 it brought a good thousand volunteers from the victorious Condor Legion home. But who's interested in that nowadays? You, Konny?

4

AT ONE OF THE MEETINGS HE SETS UP FOR US, calling them working sessions, he said the following: Properly speaking, any strand of the plot having to do directly or loosely with the city of Danzig and its environs should be his concern. For that reason, he, and no one else, should have been the one to narrate, whether briefly or at length, everything involving the ship: the circumstances of its naming, the purpose it fulfilled after the war began, and hence also its end off the Stolpe Bank. Soon after the publication of that mighty tome, *Dog Years,* this material had been dumped at his feet. He—who else?—should have been the one to dig through it, layer by layer. There had been no shortage of references to the fate of the Pokriefkes, chief among them Tulla. It was safe to assume that what was left of the family—Tulla's two older brothers had been killed in action—were among the thousands and thousands of refugees who managed to squeeze onto the overloaded *Gustloff* at the last minute, and with them the pregnant Tulla.

Unfortunately, he said, he hadn't been able to pull it off. A regrettable omission, or, to be quite frank, failure on his part. But he wasn't trying to make excuses, only to admit that around the mid-sixties he'd had it with the past, that the voracious present with its incessant nownownow had kept him from producing the mere two hundred pages... Now it was too late for him. He hadn't invented me as a surrogate, rather he had discovered me, after a long search, on the list of survivors, like a piece of lost property. Although I had a rather meager profile, I was predestined: born as the ship was sinking.

He went on to say that he was sorry about the business with my son, but how could he have known that Tulla's grandson was hiding behind the ominous home page www.blutzeuge.de, though it should probably come as no surprise that Tulla Pokriefke ended up with such a grandson. She'd always gone to extremes, and besides, as was obvious, she was not a person you could keep down. But now, he said encouragingly to his assistant, it was my turn again; I had to report on what happened with the ship after it transported some of the troops of the Condor Legion from a Spanish harbor to Hamburg.

To make a long story short, one might say: And now the war began. But we're not there yet. First the KDF ship had a lovely, leisurely summer during which it was allowed to return to the familiar Norway route for half a dozen cruises. Still without shore excursions. The majority of the passengers were workers and salaried employees from the Ruhr District and Berlin, from Hanover and Bremen. Also small groups of Germans residing abroad. The ship sailed into the Byfjord and afforded the vacationers, standing at the rail with their cameras, a view of the city of Bergen. The schedule also included the Hardangerfjord, and finally the Sognefjord, where people snapped an especially large number of pictures for their albums. Into July the midnight sun was provided as an extra, to be gaped at and stored as an experience. The cost of the five-day trip, up slightly, now came to forty-five reichsmarks.

Still the war did not begin; instead the *Gustloff* was pressed into the service of physical culture. For two weeks a peaceful gymnastics meet took place in Stockholm, the Lingiad, named after Pehr Henrik Ling, the Swedish equivalent of our Gymnastics Father Jahn, I assume. The recreation vessel became the residence for over a thousand German gymnasts, male and female, all dressed alike, among them maidens from the Labor Service, the national horizontal-bar team, but also old gentlemen who still worked out on the parallel bars, as well as gymnasts from the BDM's Faith and Beauty division, and many children drilled for mass gymnastics demonstrations.

Captain Bertram did not tie up in the harbor, but dropped anchor within view of the city. The gymnasts, male and female, were shuttled to the events in motorized lifeboats. Thus the physical culturists remained under close supervision. No incidents occurred. The documents at my disposal allow one to conclude that this special operation proved successful, furthering the cause of German-Swedish friendship. The coaches of all the branches of gymnastics received special plaques, courtesy of the King of Sweden. On 6 August 1939 the *Wilhelm Gustloff* steamed into Hamburg Harbor. The KDF cruise program resumed at once.

But then the war really did begin. That is to say, while the ship was on its last peacetime cruise to the coast of Norway, during the night from 24 to 25 August, the captain was handed a radio transmission whose text, when decoded, directed him to open a sealed envelope stored in his cabin, whereupon Captain Bertram, in accordance with Order QWA 7, had the crew abort the cruise and—without alarming the passengers with explanations—steer for the ship's home port. Four days after its arrival, the Second World War began.

That was the end of Strength through Joy. The end of holidays at sea. The end of photos and lazy chats on the sundeck. The end of good times and the end of a classless society on board. As a unit of the German Labor Front, the KDF organization devoted itself from now on to providing entertainment for all Wehrmacht units and the growing number, at first slowly, of wounded. KDF theaters became front theaters. The ships of the KDF fleet came under the command of the navy, and that included the *Wilhelm Gustloff,* outfitted as a hospital ship with five hundred beds. In place of some of the discharged peacetime crew, medics came aboard. A green stripe all around and red crosses on either side of the funnel gave the ship a new look.

Thus made recognizable in accordance with international conventions, the *Gustloff* set sail on 27 September for the Baltic, passed the islands of Sjælland and Bornholm, and after an uneventful trip tied up in Danzig-Neufahrwasser, across from the Westerplatte, recently the scene of fierce fighting. Immediately several hundred wounded Poles were brought on board, as well as ten wounded crew members from the German minesweeper *M-85*, which had run over a Polish mine in the Bay of Danzig and sunk; this, for the time being, was the sum total of German casualties.

And how did news of the beginning of the war reach the prisoner David Frankfurter, incarcerated on neutral Swiss ground, the man whose well-aimed shots had involuntarily given his victim's name to a vessel that was now a hospital ship? It can be assumed that in the daily routine of 1 September in Sennhof Prison no special events were taken note of; but from then on the behavior of the other inmates toward David Frankfurter apparently reflected fluctuations in the military situation— the stigma the Jew Frankfurter bore or the respect he enjoyed. The percentage of anti-Semites in the prison must have been approximately the same as outside its walls: a balanced proportion, taking the Helvetian Confederation as a whole.

And what was Captain Marinesko doing when first German troops marched into Poland, but then Russian soldiers as well, on the basis of the Hitler-Stalin pact? He was still commander of the 250-metric-ton *M-96*, and since he had received no orders for deployment, continued to practice rapid submersion in the eastern Baltic with his crew of eighteen. With undiminished thirst, he remained the dry-land boozer he had always been, also got involved with several women, but had not yet been subject to any disciplinary action and may well have been dreaming of a larger U-boat, equipped with more than two torpedo tubes.

Hindsight, they say, is always 20-20. In the meantime I've learned that my son did have casual contact with skinheads. Mölln had some of these types. Because of the local incident that resulted in several deaths, they were probably under surveillance, and chose other venues for opening their big mouths, such as Wismar or the sites of larger gatherings in the state of Brandenburg. In Mölln, Konny probably kept his distance, but he gave a speech in Schwerin, where he spent not only weekends but also part of his school holidays with his grandmother. The good-sized horde of skinheads, which included groups from the surrounding area in Mecklenburg, must have found his speech long-winded, for he was obliged to shorten it as he was speaking. The written text was devoted to the martyr and heroic son of Schwerin.

Yet Konny must have succeeded in winning friends for his topic among some of the local young Nazis, fixated—as usual—on hate slogans and harassing foreigners, for there was a brief period during which a local gang called itself the Wilhelm Gustloff Comrades. As I was able to ascertain later, the gathering took place in the back room of a restaurant on Schweriner Strasse.

The audience of about fifty included members of a right-wing radical party as well as interested middle-class citizens. Mother was not among them.

I am trying to picture my son, tall and spindly, with glasses and curly hair, standing there in his Norwegian sweater among those bald-headed brutes. He, the fruit juice drinker, surrounded by big bruisers armed with beer bottles. He, with his soft adolescent voice, which kept breaking, drowned out by those braggarts. He, the loner, with sweat-drenched stale air wafting around him.

No, he did not try to adapt, remained an anomaly in the midst of a crowd that normally rejected any foreign body. Hatred of Turks, beating up foreigners for fun, hurling insults at anyone not from around here—these things could not be expected of him. His speech contained no call to violent action. When he described the murder in Davos, proceeding to analyze every detail soberly, like a detective tracking down possible motives, he did allude, as on his Web site, to the murderer's presumed backers, referring to the "world Jewish conspiracy" and the Jewish-controlled plutocracy, but his manuscript did not contain abusive terms like "filthy Jew" or the exclamation "Death to the Jews!" Even his demand for a commemorative stone on the southern bank of Lake Schwerin, "in the very place where the mighty granite boulder honoring the martyr stood after 1937," was worded politely in the form of an appeal, drawing on customary democratic practice. Yet when he proposed to the audience that a citizens' petition to that effect be submitted to the Mecklenburg legislature, the response, I am told, was derisive guffaws. A pity Mother wasn't there.

Konny swallowed the rebuff and went on at once to describe the launching of the ship. He dwelt too long on the meaning and purpose of the Strength through Joy organization. On the other hand, his account of the deployment of the reoutfitted hospital ship during the occupation of Norway and Denmark by units of the Wehrmacht and navy commanded some attention among the beer drinkers, especially because several "heroes of Narvik" were among the wounded brought aboard. But then, when after the victorious campaign against France the planned invasion of England, Operation Seal, failed to come off, and instead of being deployed as a troop transport the *Gustloff* ended up boringly anchored in Gotenhafen, the boredom communicated itself to the audience.

My son found it impossible to finish his speech. Shouts of "Knock it off!" and "Cut the crap!" as well as the noise of beer bottles being banged on tables caused him to abridge his version of the ship's fateful progress toward disaster; he got only as far as the torpedoes. Konny bore this development with composure. What a good thing Mother wasn't there. The almost-sixteen-year-old probably consoled himself with the thought that he always had access to the Internet. No further contacts with skinheads are documented.

He didn't fit in with the baldies. Soon after that, Konny began to work on a report that he wanted to present orally to the teachers and students at his school in Mölln. But before he reaches that point and is refused permission to make his presentation, I need to stay on track and first give an account of the *Gustloff* in wartime: as a hospital ship it was not sufficiently in demand, and had to be converted again.

The ship was gutted. At the end of November '40 the X-ray machines disappeared. The operating rooms and the outpatient clinic were dismantled. No more nurses bustled around, no hospital beds stood in neat rows. Along with most of the civilian crew, the doctors and medics were discharged or reassigned to other ships. Of the engine-room operators, only those who serviced the engines remained. In place of the head doctor, a U-boat officer at the rank of lieutenant commander was now in charge; as commander of the Second Submarine Training Division he oversaw the functions of the "floating barracks," where sailors lived while they underwent training. Captain Bertram remained on board, but there was no course for him to plot. On the photographs at my disposal he certainly looks impressive, but he was a captain subject to recall, a second-in-command. This experienced captain from the merchant marine had a hard time adhering to military instructions, the more so since now everything on board changed. The portraits of Robert Ley were replaced by photos of the admiral of the fleet. The smoking parlor on the lower promenade deck became the officers' mess. The large dining rooms were turned into troughs for the noncommissioned officers and enlisted men. In the forecastle, dining rooms and lounges were set up for the remaining civilian crew. No longer classless, the *Wilhelm Gustloff* lay tied up at one of the piers of what had been the Polish port of Gdynia but since the beginning of the war had to be called Gotenhafen. For years the ship didn't budge from there.

Four training-division companies were billeted on board. In the papers at my disposal—which, by the way, were quoted verbatim on the Internet and disseminated with the added ingredient of visual material; my son had access to a source that is now mine—assurances are offered that as an experienced submarine commander Lieutenant Commander Wilhelm Zahn provided rigorous training for the volunteers. The U-boat sailors, younger and younger as the war progressed—toward the end seventeen-year-olds were being taken—spent four months on board. After that many of them faced certain death, whether in the Atlantic, the Mediterranean, or, later, along the northernmost route to Murmansk, where they were sent to hunt down American convoys loaded with armaments destined for the Soviet Union.

The years 1940, 1941, and 1942 came and went, producing victories tailor-made for special bulletins. While to the east whole armies were encircled, and in the Libyan desert the Africa Corps took Tobruk, nothing much happened on board, aside from the uninterrupted production of cannon fodder and the relatively safe and comfortable rear-echelon service in which the training personnel and the rest of the crew engaged (in the ship's cinema they showed Ufa's older and newer films), unless one counts the appearance of Admiral of the Fleet Dönitz during his visit to the Gotenhafen-Oxhöft docks as an event; to be sure, only official photos have been preserved.

His visit took place in March of '43. By then Stalingrad had fallen. All the front lines were receding. Since control of the skies over the Reich had been lost long since, here, too, the war was edging closer; but instead of the nearby city of Danzig, it was Gotenhafen that the American 8th Airborne Division chose as its target. The hospital ship *Stuttgart* burned. The submarine escort vessel *Eupen* was sunk. Several tugboats, as well as a Finnish and a Swedish steamer, sank after receiving direct hits. A freighter in dry dock sustained damage. The *Gustloff,* however, escaped with only a gash in the starboard hull. A bomb that detonated in the harbor had caused the damage: the ship had to be put in dry dock. On a subsequent test run in the Bay of Danzig the "swimming barracks" proved to be still seaworthy.

In the meantime, the captain in command of the ship was no longer Bertram but—as once before, in the KDF era—Petersen. There were no more victories, only reverses along all sections of the eastern front, and the Libyan desert also had to be evacuated. Fewer and fewer U-boats returned from their missions. The large cities were crumbling under the impact of surface bombing; but Danzig still stood, with all its gables and towers. In a carpentry shop in the suburb of Langfuhr, work continued unabated on doors and windows for barracks. Around this time, when not only special victory bulletins but also butter, meat, eggs, and even dried legumes were scarce, Tulla Pokriefke was called up for war service as a streetcar conductor. She was pregnant for the first time, but lost the wee one after she intentionally jumped off the car on the trip between Langfuhr and Oliva: repeatedly, and each time just before a stop, which she described to me as if it were a particular form of physical exercise.

And something else happened in the meantime. When the Swiss began to worry that their still megalomaniac neighbor might decide to occupy them, David Frankfurter was transferred from the prison in Chur to a penal institution in the French part of the country, for his protection, as the explanation went; and the commander of the 250-metric-ton submarine *M-96,* Aleksandr Marinesko, was promoted to lieutenant commander and put in charge of a new boat. Two years earlier he had sunk a cargo ship, which according to his report was a seven-thousand-tonner but according to the Soviet naval command was a ship of only eighteen hundred tons.

The new boat, *S-13,* of which Marinesko had dreamed so long, whether sober or sloshed, belonged to the Stalinetz class. Perhaps fate—no, chance—no, the strict conditions of the Treaty of Versailles—helped get him this state-of-the-art ship. After the end of the First World War, the German Reich was prohibited from building U-boats, so the Krupp-Germania Shipyard in Kiel and the engine-building company Schiffsmaschinenbau AG in Bremen took their plans to the Ingenieurs Kantoor voor Scheepsbouw in The Hague and had this company, under contract to the German navy, design an oceangoing vessel to the highest technical specifications. Later, under the aegis of German-Soviet collaboration, the newly built boat was launched in the Soviet Union, like the earlier Stalinetz boats, and was put into service as a unit of the Baltic Red Banner Fleet, shortly before the Germans' surprise attack on Russia. Whenever *S-13* left its floating base, the *Smolny,* in the Finnish harbor of Turku, it had ten torpedoes on board.

On the Web site, my son, bristling with naval expertise, voiced the opinion that the U-boat designed in Holland was a prime example of "German engineering." That may be true. But for the time being, Marinesko managed to sink an oceangoing tugboat called the *Siegfried* along the coast of Pomerania only by dint of using artillery fire. After three torpedoes failed to hit their mark, the submarine surfaced and immediately put its 10-cm guns in the bow to work.

Now let me leave the ship lying where it was relatively safe, except from air attacks, and crabwalk forward to return to my private misery. It was not as though you could tell from the beginning in what way Konny had gone astray. It looked to me like innocuous childish stuff that he was scattering as he roved through cyberspace, for instance when he compared the KDF cruises, kept inexpensive for propaganda reasons, with the package deals offered to participants in today's tourism for the masses—the cost of tickets for Caribbean cruises on so-called dream ships, or TUI offerings. Needless to say, the comparisons always worked out to the advantage of the "classless" *Gustloff,* on course to Norway, and other ships of the German Labor Front. Now *that* had been true socialism, he boasted on his Web site. The Communists had tried to get something similar going in the GDR. Unfortunately, he commented, the attempt had not succeeded. After the war they didn't even manage to complete the gigantic KDF facility of Prora, on the island of Rügen, planned in peacetime to accommodate 20,000 people for holidays at the seaside.

"Now," he asserted, "the KDF ruins must be designated a historic site!" And he went on to bicker in schoolboy fashion with his adversary David, whom I had long taken for his invention. They argued about the prospects of achieving a Volk community that would be not only nationalist but also socialist. Konny quoted Gregor Strasser, but also Robert Ley, whose ideas received from him a grade of "excellent." He spoke of a "sound Volk body," whereupon David warned him against "socialist-style pseudo-egalitarianism" and called Ley an "alcohol-sodden blowhard."

I skimmed through this chitchat, finding it only mildly amusing, and realized that the more my son raved about Strength through Joy as a brilliant project and model for the future, and praised the Workers' and Peasants' State's efforts to bring a similar socialist vacation paradise to fruition, notwithstanding all the shortages and shortcomings, the more embarrassingly I could hear his grandmother speaking through him. I no sooner entered

Konny's chat room than my ear was filled with the irrepressible jabber of the has-beens.

Mother had provoked me and others in much the same way long ago. During the period before I went to the West, I would hear her holding forth at our kitchen table in her role as Stalin's last faithful follower: "And let me tell you, comrades, you know how our Walter Ulbricht started out small as a carpenter's apprentice? Well, I started in a carpentry apprenticeship, too, and always smelled of bone glue..."

Later, after the First Secretary was forced to vacate the premises, she apparently experienced difficulties. Not because I had fled the Republic, but rather because she belittled Ulbricht's successor as a "puny roofer" and suspected revisionists under every rock. When she was summoned before the Party collective, she is said to have cited Wilhelm Gustloff as a victim of Zionism, describing him as "the tragically murdered son of our beautiful city of Schwerin."

Nonetheless, Mother managed to hang on to her position. She was both loved and feared. The recipient of several awards for "activism," she continued to fulfill quotas successfully, and up to the end remained the leader of her carpenters' brigade at the People's Own Furniture Combine on Güstrower Strasse. She also increased the number of women apprenticing as carpenters to over twenty percent.

When the Workers' and Peasants' State was gone and the Berlin Handover Trust opened a branch in Schwerin, responsible for the city and surrounding countryside,

Mother is supposed to have had her fingers in the pie, assisting with the winding down and privatizing of the People's Own Cable Works, the PlastExtrusion Machine Works, and other large manufacturing plants such as the Klement Gottwald Works, which made marine hardware, and even her own old Furniture Combine. It is safe to assume that she did not come away empty-handed from the general grabfest that took place in the East, for once the new currency arrived, Mother was not completely dependent on her pension. And when she gave my son the computer, with all the costly peripherals, the purchase did not leave her destitute. I attribute her generosity—toward me she was always fairly stingy—to an event that didn't make waves in the West German press but had a decisive influence on Konny.

But before I get around to describing the survivors' reunion, I have to bring up an embarrassing incident that a certain someone would like to talk me out of, he having formed a far too immaculate picture of his Tulla. On 30 January 1990, when that damned date seemed to have been withdrawn from circulation, because everywhere people were dancing to the tune of "Our Single German Fatherland," and all the Ossies were panting for the D-mark, Mother undertook her own kind of action.

On the southern bank of Lake Schwerin, a three-story mouse-gray youth hostel was quietly crumbling away. It had been built in the fifties and named for Kurt Bürger, an early Stalinist who had arrived from Moscow at war's end as a certified antifascist and had earned his spurs in Mecklenburg by taking a tough stance. Behind the Kurt Bürger Youth Hostel, Mother placed a bouquet of long-stemmed roses at approximately the spot overlooking the lake where the granite boulder honoring the martyr was supposed to have stood. She did this in the dark, at exactly 10:18 P.M. She later described her nocturnal act to her friend Jenny and me, giving the precise time. She was all alone, and with her flashlight had searched for the place behind the youth hostel, which was closed for the winter. For a long time she was uncertain, but then, with the sky overcast and a cold rain falling, she decided that she had found it. "But I didn't bring them flowers for Gustloff. He was just one Nazi of many that got shot down. No, it was for the ship and all them little children that died that night in the ice-cold sea. I put down that bunch of white roses at ten-eighteen on the dot. And I cried for them, forty-five years after it happened..."

Five years later, Mother was no longer alone. Herr Schön and the management of the Baltic seaside resort of Damp, along with the gentlemen from the Rescue by Sea organization, issued the invitation. Ten years earlier a reunion of survivors had taken place at the same location. In those days the Wall and the barbed wire were still in place, and no one had been allowed to come from the East German state. But this time people came who for years had not dared to mention the sinking of the ship, for political reasons. Thus it was not surprising that the guests from the new German states were greeted with particular warmth; among the survivors, there were to be no invidious distinctions made between Ossies and Wessies.

In the resort's ballroom a banner hung over the stage, proclaiming in lettering that varied in size from line to line, MEMORIAL SERVICE FOR THE 50TH ANNIVERSARY OF THE SINKING OF THE "WILHELM GUSTLOFF," DAMP ON THE BALTIC, 28–30 JANUARY 1995. No one mentioned publicly that this date happened to coincide with the takeover in '33 and the birthday of the man whom David Frankfurter had shot in order to give a sign to the Jewish people. But in smaller circles, during coffee breaks or between sessions, it was alluded to parenthetically, in an undertone.

Mother had forced me to come. She hit me over the head with an irrefutable argument: "Seeing as how it's your fiftieth, too..." She had invited our son Konrad, and when Gabi raised no objections, she carried him off in triumph. She drove up in her sand-colored Trabant, quite a sight in Damp among the gleaming Mercedes and Opels. She had ignored the request I voiced earlier that she be satisfied with me and spare Konny this wallowing in the past. As a father and in other respects, too, I simply didn't count; on this assessment of me, my mother and my ex, who otherwise had little to say to each other, agreed: to Mother, I was "a wet noodle," and Gabi never missed a chance to tell me what a failure I was.

Thus it was not surprising that the two and a half days in Damp proved quite awkward for me. I stood around at a loss, smoking like a chimney. As a reporter, of course, I could have put together a feature article on the event, or at least a news brief. Probably the organization's directors expected something of the sort from me, because Mother introduced me at first as "a reporter from them Springer papers." I didn't correct her, but the only sentence I got down on paper was, "The weather is the way it is." In whose voice could I have written a report? That of a "child of the *Gustloff*"? Or that of an objective professional?

Mother had an answer for everything. Since she recognized several other survivors among the crowd and was spontaneously approached by former crew members from the torpedo boat *Löwe,* she seized every opportunity to introduce me, if not as a Springer reporter, then as "the little boy who was born smack in the middle of the disaster." And she had to add that the thirtieth would provide an occasion to celebrate my fiftieth birthday, even though the schedule called for an hour of silent remembrance on this day.

Several births are supposed to have occurred before the ship sank, as well as on the following day, but with the exception of one person born on the twenty-ninth, no one else of my age was there in Damp. The majority of the guests were old people, because hardly any children had been saved. Among the younger survivors was a ten-year-old from Elbing, who now lives in Canada. He had been asked by the directors to describe for the audience the particulars of his rescue.

Altogether, and for obvious reasons, there are fewer and fewer witnesses to the disaster. If over five hundred survivors and rescuers had turned up for the reunion in '85, this time only two hundred had come, which caused Mother to whisper to me during the hour of remembrance, "Soon none of us will be alive anymore, only you. But you just don't want to write down all the stuff I've told you."

Yet I was the one who managed to smuggle Heinz Schön's book to her, long before the Wall came down, though admittedly to silence her gnawing reproaches. And shortly before the reunion in Damp she received from me an Ullstein paperback, written by three Englishmen. But even this documentation of the catastrophe, which I must admit was written factually but too emotionlessly, did not please her: "It's all too impersonal; nothing comes from the heart!" And then she said, when I stopped in to see her in Grosser Dreesch, "Well, maybe my Konradchen will write something about it someday..."

That explains why she took him along to Damp. She arrived, or rather made her entrance, in a black velvet ankle-length dress, buttoned up to the neck, that set off her cropped white hair. Wherever she stood, or sat over coffee and pastries, she was the center of attention. She especially drew men. As we know, she had always had that effect. Her schoolmate Jenny had told me about all the boys who stuck to her like flies during her youth; from childhood on, she is supposed to have smelled of carpenter's glue, and I could swear there was a hint of that odor about her in Damp.

But now it was old men, most of them in dark-blue suits, standing around this tough old bird in black. The stout graybeards included a former lieutenant commander who had been in charge of the torpedo boat *T-36*—its crew had rescued several hundred of the victims—and an officer who had survived the sinking of the *Gustloff*. But it was especially the crew members from the *Löwe* whose memories of Mother had remained vivid. I had the distinct impression that the men had been waiting for her. They thronged around Mother, whose demeanor took on something girlish, and could not tear themselves away. I heard her giggle, saw her cross her arms and assume a pose. But it was no longer about me and my dramatic birth at the moment of the ship's sinking; now it was all about Konny. Mother introduced my son to the older gentlemen as if he were her own; and I kept my distance, not wanting to be questioned or, worse still, celebrated by the *Löwe* veterans.

Watching from the sidelines, I noticed that Konny, who had always seemed rather shy, handled himself confidently in the role Mother had assigned him, giving brief but clear answers, asking questions, listening intently, venturing a youthful laugh now and then, even standing still to have his picture taken. At almost fifteen—his birthday would come in March—he showed not a trace of childishness, instead appeared ripe for Mother's plan of initiating him into the complete story of the disaster and, as would become apparent, having him promulgate the legend.

From then on, everything revolved around him. Although one survivor in attendance had been born on the *Gustloff* the day before the boat sank, and he, like me, was given his own copy of Schön's book by the author—the mothers were honored on stage with bouquets—it seemed to me as though all this was done merely to impress Konny's obligation upon him. People were placing their hopes in him. Great things were expected of our Konny. He would not let the survivors down.

Mother had stuck him in a dark-blue suit, which called for a collegiate tie. With his glasses and curly hair, he looked like a cross between an archangel and a boy at First Communion. He presented himself as if he had a mission, as if he were about to proclaim something sacred, as if he had been vouchsafed a revelation.

The service of remembrance took place at the hour when the torpedoes struck the ship. I don't know who suggested that Konrad sound the ship's bell, hung next to the altar; in the late seventies Polish divers had salvaged it from the aft of the wreck's upper deck. Now, on the occasion of this survivors' reunion, the crew of the salvage vessel *Szkwal* had presented their found object to signal Polish-German rapprochement. But in the end it was Herr Schön after all who was allowed to strike the bell three times with a hammer to mark the end of the service.

The purser's assistant on the *Gustloff* was eighteen when the ship went down. I do not want to conceal the fact that in Damp little gratitude was expressed to this man who after the disaster had collected and researched almost everything he could track down. At the beginning of the reunion he spoke on the topic "The Sinking of the *Wilhelm Gustloff* on 30 January 1945 from the Russians' Perspective." In the course of his speech, it became evident that he had visited the Soviet Union often to do his research, had made the acquaintance of a petty officer from the U-boat *S-13,* and, what is more, had remained in friendly contact with this Vladimir Kourotchkin, who, on his commander's orders, had sent the three torpedoes speeding on their way, and had even been photographed shaking hands with the old man. With these revelations, he had, as Schön later reticently put it, "lost some friends."

After the speech, they cut him dead. From then on, many in the audience labeled him a Russian-lover. For them the war had not ended. The Russian was still "Ivan," the three torpedoes murder weapons. But from Vladimir Kourotchkin's point of view, the nameless ship he sank had been stuffed to the gills with Nazis, responsible for launching a surprise attack on his homeland and leaving scorched earth when they retreated. Not until he met Schön did he learn that after the torpedoes hit their mark, more than four thousand children drowned, froze to death, or were sucked into the depths with the ship. The petty officer apparently dreamed of those children for a long time afterward, always the same dream.

For Heinz Schön, being allowed to strike the bell after all did help soften the slights he had suffered. But my son, who on his home page introduced the Russian who fired the torpedoes, paired in a photo with the *Gust-loff* researcher, commented that this tragedy had brought two peoples together by virtue of its lasting effects; he pointed to the origin of the U-boat, with its sure aim, citing the "superb German engineering," and even went so far as to assert that only a boat built to German specifications could have brought the Soviets such success that day off the Stolpe Bank.

And I? After the service of remembrance I slunk away to the beach, now shrouded in darkness. There I paced back and forth. Alone, my mind completely blank. Since no wind was blowing, the Baltic lapped the shore listlessly, bearing no message.

5

THIS BUSINESS HAS BEEN GNAWING AT THE OLD BOY.
Actually, he says, his generation should have been the
one. It should have found words for the hardships
endured by the Germans fleeing East Prussia: the westward treks in the depths of winter, people dying in
blinding snowstorms, expiring by the side of the road or
in holes in the ice when the frozen bay known as the
Frisches Haff began to break up under the weight of
horse-drawn carts after being hit by bombs, and still,
from the direction of Heiligenbeil, more and more
people streaming across the endless snowy waste, terri-
fied of Russian reprisal . . . fleeing . . . white death . . . Never,
he said, should his generation have kept silent about
such misery, merely because its own sense of guilt was so
overwhelming, merely because for years the need to accept responsibility and show remorse took precedence,
with the result that they abandoned the topic to the right
wing. This failure, he says, was staggering . . .

But now the old man, who has worn himself out writing, thinks he has found in me someone who has no

choice but to stand in for him and report on the incursion of the Soviet armies into the Reich, on Nemmersdorf, and the consequences. It's true: I'm searching for the right words. But he's not the one forcing me to do this, it's Mother. And it's only because of her that the old man is poking his nose in; she's forcing him to force me, as if all this could be written only under duress, as if nothing could get down on paper without Mother.

He claims that in the days when he knew her she was an inscrutable person, someone you could never pin down to any opinion. He wants my Tulla to have this same diffuse glow, and is disappointed now. Never, he says, would he have thought that the Tulla Pokriefke who survived the disaster would have developed in such a banal direction, turning into a Party functionary and an "activist" obediently fulfilling her quotas. He would have expected something anarchistic of her instead, an irrational act, such as setting off a bomb without a specific motive, or perhaps coming to some horrifying realization. After all, he says, it was the adolescent Tulla who, in the middle of wartime and surrounded by people deliberately turning a blind eye, saw a whitish heap to one side of the Kaiserhafen flak battery, recognized it as human remains, and announced loudly, "That's a pile o' bones!"

The old man doesn't really know Mother. And I? Do I know her any better? Probably only Aunt Jenny has any inkling of her being—or nothingness; at one point she told me, "Fundamentally my friend Tulla should be seen as a nun manqué, with stigmata, of course..." This much is clear: Mother is impossible to read. Even as a Party cadre she could not be made to toe the line. When I wanted to go to the West, her only response was, "Well, go on over, for all I care," and she didn't blow the whistle on me, with the result that considerable pressure was put on her in Schwerin; even the Stasi is supposed to have come knocking, but apparently without success...

In those days she placed all her hopes in me. But then I fizzled out, and she decided I was a waste of time, so as soon as the Wall was gone, she began to knead my son. Konny was only ten or eleven when he fell into his grandmother's clutches. And after the survivors' reunion in Damp, where I was a nonentity, lurking on the edges while he became the crown prince, she pumped him full of tales: tales of the flight, of atrocities, of rapes—tales about things she hadn't experienced in person but that were being told everywhere once Russian tanks rolled across the eastern border of the Reich in October 1944 and advanced into the districts of Goldab and Gumbin-nen, tales that spread like wildfire, causing terror and panic.

That's how it must have—could have been. That's more or less the way it was. When units of the German 4th Army managed to retake the town of Nemmersdorf a few days after the advance of the Soviet 11th Guards Army, one could smell, see, count, photograph, and film for the newsreels shown in all the cinemas in the Reich how many women had been raped by Russian soldiers, then killed and nailed to barn doors. T-34 tanks had pursued people as they fled and rolled over them. Children who had been shot were left lying in front gardens and in ditches. Even French prisoners of war, who had been forced to work on farms near Nemmersdorf, were liquidated—forty of them, so the story went.

These particulars and others as well I found on the Internet under the address with which I was by now familiar. There was also a translation of an appeal penned by the Russian writer Ilya Ehrenburg, calling on all Russian soldiers to murder, rape, and take revenge for the havoc wreaked by the fascist beasts on the fatherland, revenge for Mother Russia. Under the URL www.blutzeuge.de my son, recognizable only to me, bewailed this state of affairs in the language used during the period in question for official proclamations: "These horrors were visited by subhuman Russians on defenseless German women..." and "Thus the Russian soldateska raged..." and "This terror still menaces all of Europe if no dam is erected against the Asiatic tide..." As an added attraction he had scanned and included a poster used by the German Christian Democrats in the fifties, showing a devouring monster with Asiatic features.

Spread by way of the Internet and downloaded by who knows how many users, these sentences and the captions to the accompanying illustrations could be read as if they applied to current events, even though the crumbling of Russia or the atrocities in the Balkans and in Ruanda were not mentioned. To illustrate his latest campaign, my son needed no more than the corpse-strewn battlefields of the past; no matter who had sown them, they bore a rich harvest.

The only thing left for me to add is that during those few days when Nemmersdorf became the epitome of horror, the contempt for everything Russian that had previously been instilled in Germans abruptly turned into abject fear of the Russians themselves. The newspaper reports, radio commentaries, and newsreel images from the reconquered town triggered a mass exodus from East Prussia, which escalated into panic when the Soviets launched their major offensive in mid-January. As people fled by land, they began to die like flies by the side of the road. I can't describe it. No one can describe it. Just this: some of the refugees reached the ports of Pillau, Danzig, and Gotenhafen. Hundreds of thousands tried to escape by ship from the horror closing in on them. Hundreds of thousands—the statistics tell us over two million made it safely to the West—crowded onto warships, passenger liners, and freighters. So, too, people crowded onto the *Wilhelm Gustloff,* which had been lying at Gotenhafen's Oxhöft Pier for years.

I wish I could make things as easy for myself as my son, who proclaimed on his Web site, "In a calm and orderly fashion the ship took on the girls and women, mothers and children fleeing before the Russian beast..." Why did he suppress any reference to the thousand U-boat sailors and the 370 members of the naval women's auxiliary, likewise the crews of the hastily dismantled flak batteries? He did mention in passing that at the beginning and toward the end some wounded were brought on board—"Among them were fighters from the Kurland front, which was still holding against the onslaught of the red tide..."—but in his account of the conversion of the barracks ship into a seaworthy transport vessel, he noted with pedantic precision how many tons of flour and powdered milk, how many slaughtered swine came on board, but said not a word about the Croatian volunteer soldiers pressed into duty, without sufficient training, to supplement the ship's crew. Not a word about the ship's inadequate radio system. Not a word about the emergency drill—"Close watertight doors!" It is understandable that he emphasized the foresight that went into setting up a delivery room, but what kept him from even hinting that his grandmother was in the advanced stages of pregnancy? And not a word about the ten missing lifeboats, which had been commandeered for spreading a smoke screen in the harbor during air raids, and replaced by smaller-capacity rowboats and hastily stacked and roped-together life rafts, filled with compacted kapok. The *Gustloff* was to be presented to Internet users as a refugee ship only.

Why did Konny lie? Why did the boy deceive himself and others? Why, when he was otherwise such a stickler for detail, and knew every inch of the ship, from the shaft tunnel to the most remote corner of the onboard laundry, did he refuse to admit that it was neither a Red Cross transport nor a cargo ship that lay tied up at the dock, loaded exclusively with refugees, but an armed passenger liner under the command of the navy, into which the most varied freight had been packed? Why did he deny facts available in print for years, facts that even the eternal has-beens hardly contested anymore? Did he want to fabricate a war crime and impress the skinheads in Germany and elsewhere with a prettied-up version of what had actually happened? Was his emotional need for clear-cut victims so compelling that his Web site could not accommodate even an appearance by the civilian Captain Petersen's military nemesis, Lieutenant Commander Zahn, accompanied by his German shepherd?

I can only suspect what induced Konny to cheat: the desire for an unambiguous enemy. But the story about the dog I have straight from Mother as actual fact; even as a child she was fixated on German shepherds. Zahn had had his Hassan on board for years. Whether on deck or in the mess, the officer always appeared with his dog in tow. Mother said, "From down on the dock—where we had to wait before they let us on—we could see clearly a captain or some such standing up there at the railing with that pooch of his and looking down at us refugees. The dog was almost exactly like our Harras..."

She could also describe the situation on the dock: "You wouldn't believe the pushing and shoving, total confusion. In the beginning they were keeping a neat list—everyone who came up the gangway—but then the paper ran out..." So the numbers will forever remain uncertain. But what do numbers tell us? Numbers are never accurate. In the end you always have to guess.

Among the 6,600 persons recorded were a good 5,000 refugees. But from 28 January on, additional hordes of people, who were no longer being counted, stormed up the gangplank. Was it two or three thousand, destined to remain numberless and nameless? Approximately that number of extra meal cards was printed on board and distributed by the girls of the naval auxiliary, who had been pressed into service. It didn't matter, and still doesn't, if there were a few hundred more or less. No one has precise figures. It is not known either how many baby carriages were stowed in the hold; and it can only be estimated that in the end the ship held close to four and a half thousand infants, children, and youths.

Finally, when no more was possible, a few last wounded and a final squad of women's auxiliaries were squeezed in, the young girls being billeted in the emptied swimming pool on E deck, below the ship's waterline, because no more cabins were available, and all the lounges were already filled with mattresses.

This specific location must be repeated and emphasized, because my son breathed not a word about anything connected with the naval auxiliaries and the swimming pool as a death trap. Only when he waxed indignant on his Web site about rapes, did he speak, almost rhapsodically, of the "young maidens whose innocence was supposed to be protected by the ship from the depredations of the Russian beast..."

When I came upon this nonsense, I again took action, but without identifying myself as his father. When his chat room opened, I lobbed in my objections: "Your maidens in distress were wearing uniforms, attractive ones, even. Knee-length grayish-blue skirts and close-fitting jackets. Their caps, with the imperial eagle gripping the swastika in front, perched rakishly atop their hairdos. All of them, whether innocent or not, had undergone military training and had sworn the loyalty oath to their Führer..."

But my son didn't care to communicate with me. Only with his invented adversary, whom he lectured in the tone of a classic racist: "As a Jew you will never be able to grasp how much the violation of German girls and women by Kalmucks, Tatars, and other Mongol types still hurts. But what would you Jews know about purity of the blood!"

That couldn't be something Mother had drummed into him. Or could it? Not so long ago, when I had visited her in Grosser Dreesch and had laid on her coffee table my fairly objective article on the controversy over the proposed Holocaust memorial in Berlin, she told me about someone who once turned up at her uncle's carpentry shop, "a fat kid with freckles" who drew a fairly good likeness of the dog lying chained up there: "He was a Yid, and he had some weird notions. But he was only half Jewish, so my papa said. And he said it out loud, too, before he kicked that Yid—Amsel was his name—out of our courtyard..."

On the morning of the thirtieth, Mother finally managed to get on board, with her parents. "We was just in the nick of time..." They lost some of their luggage in the process. At noon the order arrived for the *Gustloff* to raise anchor and cast off. Hundreds were left behind on the pier.

"Mama and Papa were ashamed of me, of course, with my big belly. Every time one of the other refugees asked about me, Mama would say, 'Her fiancé's fighting at the front.' Or: 'There was supposed to be a long-distance wedding with her fiancé, who's fighting on the western front. If only he hasn't been killed.' But to me all they talked about was the shame. It was good they separated us right away on the ship. Mama and Papa had to go way down into the belly of the ship, where there was still a bit of room left. I was sent up to the maternity ward..."

But we haven't reached that point yet. Again I have to do a little crabwalk in order to move forward: the previous day, and then all through a long night, the Pokriefkes sat on their too many suitcases and bundles, in the midst of a crowd of refugees, most of them exhausted from the long trek. They came from the Kurische Nehrung, from the Samland Peninsula, from Masuria. A last batch had fled from nearby Elbing; Russian tanks had rolled through, but the fighting for control seemed to continue. Also more and more women and children from Danzig, Zoppot, and Gotenhafen crowded in among the horse-drawn carts, farm wagons, baby carriages, and many sleighs. Mother told me about abandoned dogs who weren't allowed on board and because they were hungry made the piers unsafe. The East Prussian farm horses had been unharnessed and either turned over to the Wehrmacht units in the city or sent to the slaughterhouse. Mother didn't know exactly. But it was only the dogs she felt compassion for: "They bayed all night long like wolves..."

When the Pokriefkes left Elsenstrasse, their relatives the Liebenaus refused to pack up and follow the helper's family. The master carpenter was too attached to his workbenches, his circular and band saws, the finishing machine, the stacks of lumber in the shed, and apartment house 19, which belonged to him. His son Harry, whom Mother implicated temporarily as my possible father, had already received his call-up notice the previous fall. Somewhere, along one of the many retreating fronts, he must have been a radio operator or a member of the armored infantry.

After the war I learned that the Poles had expelled my possible grandfather and his wife, like all Germans who had remained in the region. We heard that both of them died not long afterward in the West, one right after the other, most likely in Lüneburg—he probably out of sorrow for his lost shop and all the window and door hardware stored in the apartment house's cellar. The watchdog, in whose kennel Mother is supposed to have spent a week as a child, was dead long since; before the war someone—she says, "A pal of the Yid's"—poisoned him.

It can be assumed that the Pokriefkes came aboard with one of the last lots, allowed on because their daughter was visibly pregnant. With August Pokriefke might there have been trouble; the MPs patrolling the pier could have pulled him out as fit for the Volkssturm. But since he, as Mother said, was only "a half-pint," he managed to bluff his way through. At the end, supervision became porous in any case. Conditions were chaotic. Children ended up on board without their mothers. And mothers lost hold of their children's hands in the shoving on the gangway and couldn't save them from being pushed over the edge and disappearing into the water between ship's hull and the wall of the pier. It did no good to scream.

The Pokriefkes might have found room on the steamers *Oceania* and *Antonio Delfino* instead, although they too were overloaded with refugees. These two ships were also tied up at the Gotenhafen-Oxhöft pier, known as the Quay of Good Hope; and the two medium-sized transports did reach their destinations, Kiel and Copenhagen, safely. But Erna Pokriefke was "determined" to get onto the *Gustloff*, "come hell or high water," because she had such happy memories of her KDF cruise to the Norwegian fjords on what was in those days a gleaming white ship. She had stuffed into her luggage the photo album with snapshots from that trip.

Erna and August Pokriefke must have found it hard to recognize the ship's interior, for all the reception areas and dining rooms, the library, the Folk Costume Lounge, and the Music Room had been emptied, stripped of all pictures on the walls, and reduced to mattress encampments. Even the glassed-in promenade deck and the corridors were crammed with people. Since thousands of children, both counted and uncounted, constituted part of the ship's human freight, their crying mixed with the blare of the loudspeakers, which were constantly announcing the names of lost boys and girls.

When the Pokriefkes came on board, without being recorded, Mother was separated from her parents. A nurse made the decision. We will never know whether the couple was jammed by the naval auxiliaries on duty into an already occupied cabin or whether they found a spot in a mass dormitory, along with what remained of their luggage. Tulla Pokriefke would never see the photo album and her parents again. I use this order deliberately, because I am fairly certain that the loss of the photo album was especially painful for Mother, for with it were lost all the pictures, shot with the family Kodak box camera, of her with her curly-haired brother Konrad on the boardwalk in Zoppot, with her girlfriend Jenny and Jenny's adoptive father, Dr. Brunies, in front of the Gutenberg monument in the Jäschkental Forest, as well as several with Harras, the pure-blooded German shepherd and famous breeding dog.

When Mother came to the part in her neverending story about going aboard the ship, she always talked about being in her eighth month. Probably it was the eighth. No matter which month, she was assigned to the maternity ward. It was located next to the so-called Bower, where the critically wounded soldiers were groaning, packed in like sardines. During KDF times, the Bower had been popular with the cruise participants as a sort of winter garden. It was located under the bridge. The ship's physician, Dr. Richter, chief medical officer of the Second Submarine Training Division, oversaw the

Bower as well as the maternity ward. Every time Mother told me about getting on board, she said, "It was so nice and warm there. And I got hot milk right away, too, with a nice dollop of honey in it..."

It must have been business as usual in the maternity ward. Since the beginning of the embarkation process, four babies had been born, "all little shavers," as I was told.

Some say that the *Wilhelm Gustloff* had the misfortune of having too many captains. That may be true. But the *Titanic* had only one, and even so things went wrong on its maiden voyage. Mother says that shortly before the ship pulled away from the dock, she wanted to stretch her legs, and somehow wandered onto the bridge, without being stopped by the guards—"It was only one flight up." There she saw "this old sea dog having a real knock-down-drag-out with another fellow with a goatee..."

The sea dog was Captain Friedrich Petersen, a civilian who in peacetime had held the command on several passenger liners, including the *Gustloff* for a short period, and after the outbreak of war had been captured by the British as a blockade runner. But then the British decided that because of his age he couldn't possibly be fit for military service, and once he had sworn in writing that he would never again take to the seas as a captain, he was deported to Germany. That was why this man in his mid-sixties had been assigned as a "stationary captain" to the "floating barracks" at the Oxhöft Quay.

The one with the goatee must have been Lieutenant

Commander Wilhelm Zahn, who always had his German shepherd Hassan at his heel. The former U-boat commander, whose career had been only moderately successful, was supposed to serve as the military transportation officer for the ship loaded with refugees. In addition, to support the elderly captain, whose seagoing instincts were rusty by now, two more captains, young but experienced in sailing the Baltic, also occupied the bridge; their names were Köhler and Weller. Both had been brought over from the merchant marine, and were therefore treated with considerable disdain by the naval officers, chief among them Zahn; the two groups ate in different officers' messes and talked to each other only when absolutely necessary.

Thus the bridge harbored tensions, but also shared responsibility for the ship's hard-to-define freight: on the one hand the ship was a troop transport, on the other a refugee and hospital ship. With its coat of gray paint, the *Gustloff* offered an ambiguous target. For the moment it was still safe in the harbor, except from possible air attacks. For the moment the inevitable friction among the too many captains had not yet produced a conflagration. For the moment yet another captain was completely unaware of this ship carrying children and soldiers, mothers and naval women's auxiliaries, and equipped with antiaircraft guns.

Until the end of December, *S-13* lay in the dock of the Red Banner Fleet's floating Smolny base. Once the ship had been serviced, refueled, provisioned, and loaded with torpedoes, it was ready to set out on a mission, but the commander was missing.

Alcohol and women prevented Aleksandr Marinesko from breaking off his shore leave and being on board in time for the major offensive slated to roll over the Baltic and East Prussia. As the story goes, *pontikka,* Finnish potato schnapps, had knocked him off an even keel and wiped out all memory of his obligations. He was searched for in brothels and other dives known to the military police, but in vain; the boat's captain had gone missing.

Not until 3 January did Marinesko, by now sober again, report back to Turku. The NKVD immediately interrogated him, holding him under suspicion of espionage. Since he had no recollection of any of the stages of his extended shore leave, he had nothing but memory gaps to present in his own defense. Eventually his superior, Captain First Class Orjel, managed to postpone the convening of a court-martial by citing Comrade Stalin's recent order for an all-out effort. Captain Orjel had only a few experienced commanders at his disposal and did not want to diminish the fighting power of his unit. When even the crew of *S-13* intervened in the proceedings against their captain with a petition for clemency, and the NKVD began to see mutiny as a possibility, Orjel ordered this U-boat commander, who was unreliable only on shore leave, to set course at once for Hangö, whose harbor *S-13* left a week later. Icebreakers had opened the navigation channel. The boat was supposed to head for the Baltic coast, passing the Swedish island of Gotland.

———

There is a film in black and white made at the end of the fifties. It is called *Night Fell over Gotenhafen,* and its cast includes stars like Brigitte Horney and Sonja Ziemann. The director, a German American by the name of Frank Wisbar, who had earlier made a film about Stalingrad, hired the *Gustloff* expert Heinz Schön as an adviser. Banned in the East, the film achieved only modest success in the West, and is now forgotten, like the unfortunate ship itself, submerged in the depths of archives.

While I was living with Mother's friend Jenny Brunies in West Berlin and attending secondary school, I went to see it, at her insistence—"Tulla conveyed to me that she would very much like us to see the film together"—and was quite disappointed. The plot was utterly predictable. Just as in all the *Titanic* films, a love story had to be brought in as filler, taking on heroic dimensions at the end, as if the sinking of an overcrowded ship weren't exciting, the thousands of deaths not tragic enough.

A wartime romance. In *Night Fell over Gotenhafen,* after a much too long prelude in Berlin, East Prussia, and elsewhere, the love triangle is revealed: the cuckolded husband, a soldier at the eastern front, who is later brought onto the ship, critically wounded; the unfaithful wife, a temptress torn between two men, who manages to get on board with her infant; and a playboy naval officer who figures as adulterer, father, and rescuer of the infant. Although Aunt Jenny managed to cry at certain passages in the film, when she invited me afterward to join her at the Paris Bar, where I had my first Pernod, she remarked, "Your mother would not have found much to like about the film, because they show not a single birth, either before or after the sinking of the ship..." And then she added, "In point of fact there's no way you can film something so terrible."

I'm sure that Mother didn't have a lover on board, or any of my possible fathers. It's not out of the question, however, that even in her advanced state of pregnancy she attracted men from the ship's personnel—that was her way, and still is: she possesses an internal magnet that she refers to as "a certain something." As the story goes, the anchors had hardly been weighed when one of the naval recruits, in training for U-boat duty—"A pale fellow with pimples all over his face"—escorted the pregnant girl to the top deck. She was feeling too restless to stay put. I would reckon the sailor was about Mother's age, seventeen or barely eighteen. He carefully guided her on his arm across the sundeck, which was slippery as glass, because it was completely iced over. And when Mother looked around, with those eyes that never missed a thing, she noticed that the davits, blocks, and mountings of the port and starboard lifeboats and their cables were coated with ice.

How many times have I heard her comment: "When I saw that, my knees went weak"? And in Damp, as she stood there, lean and all in black, surrounded by older gentlemen and initiating my son Konrad into the myopic world of the survivors, I heard her saying, "I realized then there was no way we could be rescued with them boats iced over. I wanted to get off. I screamed like a maniac. But it was too late already..."

The film I saw with Aunt Jenny in a theater on Kantstrasse showed none of this—no lumps of ice on the davits, no ice-coated railing, not even ice floes in the harbor. Yet in Schön's account, as well as in the paperback report by the Englishmen Dobson, Miller, and Payne, we read that on 30 January 1945 the weather was frigid—minus 18° Celsius. Icebreakers had had to clear a channel in the Bay of Danzig. Heavy seas and squalls were predicted.

When I let myself wonder nevertheless whether Mother might not have left the ship in time, the basis for this essentially pointless speculation can be found in the established fact that soon after the *Gustloff* pulled away from the dock, a coastal steamer, the *Reval,* suddenly materialized out of the driving snow, heading straight for the *Gustloff.* Crammed with refugees from Tilsit and Königsberg, the ship was coming from Pillau, the last harbor in East Prussia. Since there was not enough room belowdecks for all the passengers, they were packed in tight on the open deck. As would become clear later, many had frozen to death during the crossing but remained upright, held in place by the standing block of ice.

When the *Gustloff* stopped and let down a few rope ladders, some survivors managed to scramble to what they thought was safety on the large ship; they found crannies in the overheated corridors and stairwells.

Couldn't Mother have gone in the opposite direction by way of a rope ladder? All her life, she has known when to turn back. This would have been her chance!

Why not leave the doomed ship for the *Reval*? If she had ventured down the ladder, in spite of her big belly, I would have been born somewhere else—who knows where—but certainly later, and not on 30 January.

There it is again, that damned date. History, or, to be more precise, the history we Germans have repeatedly mucked up, is a clogged toilet. We flush and flush, but the shit keeps rising. For instance, this accursed thirtieth. How it clings to me, marks me. What good has it done that I have always avoided celebrating my birthday— whether as a schoolboy or a university student, as a news- paper editor or husband, whether among friends, col- leagues, or family members? I was always afraid that at a party someone might pin the thrice-cursed significance of the thirtieth on me—in a toast, for example—even when it looked as though this date, once force-fed to the point of bursting, had slimmed down over the years, be- coming innocuous, a day on the calendar like any other. By now, after all, we Germans have come up with ex- pressions to help us deal with the past: we are to atone for it, come to terms with it, go through a grieving process.

But then it seemed as if on the Internet flags had to be displayed—still, or again—on the thirtieth, the state holiday. At any rate, my son highlighted the day of the Nazi takeover as a red-letter day, for all the world to see. In the housing project in Grosser Dreesch, built of con- crete slabs, where he had been living with his grand- mother since the beginning of the new school year, he continued his activity as Webmaster. Gabi, my ex, had not wanted to interfere with our son's desire to exchange left-leaning maternal lecturing for grandmotherly brainwashing. Even worse, she had shrugged off all responsibility: "Konrad's going to be seventeen soon, old enough to make choices for himself."

No one thought to ask me. The two of them parted "amicably," I was told. The move from Mölln's lake to Schwerin's took place quietly. Even the change of schools supposedly went smoothly, "thanks to his above-average record," although I had a hard time picturing my son in the stagnant atmosphere of the Ossie schools. "Your prejudices are showing," Gabi commented. "Konny prefers the structured environment there to our more lax one." Then my ex put on a show of detachment: although as an educator who advocated freedom of choice and open discussion she was disappointed, as a mother she had to support her son's decision. Even Konny's girlfriend—that was how I learned of the shadowy existence of the dental assistant—could understand the step he had taken. Rosi herself planned to stay in Ratzeburg, but looked forward to visiting Konrad as often as possible.

His partner in dialogue, too, remained faithful. David, the invented or real-life provider of cues, did not object to the move, or remained unaware of it. At any rate, when the subject of the thirtieth came up in my son's chat room, he resurfaced after a fairly long absence, still spouting his antifascist sentiments. In general, the chatting had become polyphonic: protest-laden or blindly assenting. At times the babble was deafening. Soon the appointment of the Führer to the chancellorship was not the only subject of contention; now Wilhelm Gustloff's birthday was thrown into the mix. Disagreement raged over the "dispensation of Providence," as Konny insisted on calling it, that had caused the martyr prophetically to come into the world on the very date that would later mark the takeover.

This historical sleight of hand was presented to all the chatters as evidence that the events in question were predestined. Whereupon the actual or merely invented David mocked the Goliath who had been stopped dead in Davos: "So I suppose it was also Providence when the ship named after your puny Party functionary began to sink with all hands on board, on his birthday—which was also the twelfth anniversary of Hitler's putsch—and in fact at the very minute when Gustloff was born; it was exactly 9:16 in the evening when the three blasts occurred..."

They played their roles as if it had all been rehearsed. Yet I was becoming increasingly dubious about my assumption that the David who clicked into the chat room from time to time was an invention, that a homunculus was jabbering preprogrammed statements such as, "You Germans will always have Auschwitz on your brow as a mark of shame..." or, "You're a clear example yourself of the evil that is coming to the surface again..." or sentences in which David hid behind the plural: "We Jews are condemned to neverending lamentation," "We Jews never forget!" To which Wilhelm would respond with statements straight from the primer of racism, asserting that the "world Jewish conspiracy" was everywhere, but particularly powerful on New York's Wall Street.

The conflict raged relentlessly. But now and then the two would fall out of character, for instance when my son, as Wilhelm, praised the Israeli army for its toughness, while David condemned the Jewish settlements on Palestinian soil as "territorial aggression." It could also happen that they suddenly agreed with each other as they expertly discussed Ping-Pong tournaments. Thus their individual utterances, sometimes harsh, at other times chummy, revealed that two young people had found each other in cyberspace who, for all their hostile posturing, might have become friends. For example, when David logged on with something like this: "Hello there, you bristly Nazi swine! This is your Jewish sow, ripe for the slaughter, with some tips on how you might celebrate the Nazi takeover today: first put on your broken record..." Or when Wilhelm attempted to be witty: "That's enough Jewish blood spilled for today. Your favorite German chef, who loves whipping up a nice kosher brown gravy for you, is going to say bye-bye for now and log out."

Otherwise the two of them came up with nothing new on the subject of the thirtieth. Konny did have one fact with which he surprised his bosom enemy: "Did you know that our beloved Führer's last speech was broadcast on all decks of the doomed ship over the PA system?"

That was true. On the *Gustloff,* wherever loudspeakers were mounted, Hitler's speech to his people over

Greater German Radio was heard. In the maternity ward, where Mother had been advised by the head nurse to lie down on a cot, she heard that unmistakable voice proclaim, "Twelve years ago, on 30 January 1933, a truly historic day, Providence placed the destiny of the German Volk in my hands..."

Then Koch, the Gauleiter of East Prussia, spouted a dozen slogans about staying the course. Tragic music followed. But Mother mentioned only the Führer's speech: "It sure gave me the creeps when the Führer went on that way about destiny and stuff like that..." And sometimes, after falling silent for a moment, she would add, "It sounded like what you'd hear at a funeral."

But I'm getting ahead of myself. The broadcast didn't come until later. For now the ship was steaming across the relatively calm Bay of Danzig toward the tip of the Hela Peninsula.

The thirtieth fell on a Tuesday. Despite the ship's having been docked for years, the engines ran smoothly. A choppy sea and snow flurries. Soup and bread were doled out on all the enclosed decks to those with meal tickets. The two torpedo-interception boats that were supposed to escort the ship safely to Hela soon found they could not make any headway against the increasingly heavy seas and had to be authorized by radio to turn back. Also by radio came instructions as to the ship's final destination: in Kiel the future U-boat crewmen of the 2nd Training Division, the wounded, and the naval auxiliaries were to disembark or be carried off the ship; the refugees would continue on to Flensburg. Snow was still falling. The first cases of seasickness were reported. When the *Hansa,* likewise crammed with refugees, hove into view in the Hela roadstead, the convoy was complete, with the exception of the three escort boats that had been promised. But then an order was received to drop anchor.

I don't want to go into all the circumstances that caused the doomed ship—forgotten by the entire world, or, to be more accurate, repressed, but now suddenly roaming the Internet like a ghost ship—to continue its journey eventually without the *Hansa,* whose engines were damaged. The *Gustloff* was accompanied by only two escort vessels, of which one was soon called back. Just this much: the engines had hardly started up again when the quarreling broke out on the bridge as to who was in charge. The four captains were arguing with and against each other. Petersen and his first officer—also from the merchant marine—insisted that the ship travel no faster than twelve knots. The reason: after being docked so long, it should not be pushed to do more. But Zahn, the former U-boat commander, fearing enemy attacks from a firing position with which he was very familiar, wanted to increase the speed to fifteen knots. Petersen prevailed. Then the first officer, supported by the navigation captains Köhler and Weller, proposed that from Rixhöft they follow the coastal route, which was mined but shallow enough so they would be safe from U-boats. But Petersen, now supported by Zahn, decided in favor of the deep-water channel, which had been swept for mines. He rejected, however, the advice from all the other captains that the ship steer a zigzag course. The only thing not subject to dispute was the weather report: wind west-northwest at a force of six to seven, turning westerly and falling to five as evening approached. The swell at four, driving snow, visibility one to three nautical miles, medium frost.

Of all this—the continuing arguments on the bridge, the absence of an adequate number of escort vessels, and the increased icing over of everything on the upper deck—the antiaircraft guns had become inoperable—Mother remained oblivious. She recalled that after the "Führer's speech" she received from Nurse Helga five pieces of zwieback and a bowl of rice pudding with sugar and cinnamon. From the nearby Bower the groaning of the critically wounded could be heard. Fortunately the radio was playing dance music, "cheerful tunes." She fell asleep to the sound. No contractions yet. After all, Mother thought she was in her eighth month.

The *Gustloff* was not alone as it steamed along at a distance of twelve nautical miles from the Pomeranian coast. The Soviet submarine *S-13* was following the same course. The submarine had waited in vain in the waters near the embattled port city of Memel, along with two other units of the Baltic Red Banner Fleet, for ships departing or bringing reinforcements to the remnants of the German 4th Army. For days nothing came into view. While he waited, the captain of *S-13* may have been brooding over the impending court-martial and the interrogation he would have to undergo at the hands of the NKVD.

When Aleksandr Marinesko received word over the radio in the early morning hours of 30 January that the Red Army had captured Memel's port, he issued an order for a new course without informing his central command. While the *Gustloff* was still docked at the Oxhöft quay, taking on a few more batches of refugees— now the Pokriefkes came on board—*S-13,* with forty-seven men and ten torpedoes, made for the Pomeranian coast.

While in my report two boats are coming closer and closer but nothing decisive has happened yet, an opportunity offers itself for taking note of routine conditions in a Graubünden penal institution. On that Tuesday, as on every workday, the prisoners were sitting at their looms. By this time the murderer of the former Nazi Landesgruppenleiter Wilhelm Gustloff had served nine years of his eighteen-year sentence. With the war situation now radically altered—since the Greater German Reich no longer represented a threat, he had been transferred back to Sennhof Prison in Chur—he thought the moment had come for submitting a request for clemency; but it was rejected by the Swiss Supreme Court around the time of the ships' maneuvering in the Baltic. It was not only David Frankfurter but also the ship named after his victim that found no mercy.

6

HE SAYS MY REPORT WOULD MAKE A GOOD NOVELLA. A literary assessment with which I can't concern myself. I merely report the following: on the day that Providence, or some other calendar maker, had selected as the ship's last, the downfall of the Greater German Reich had already been rung in. Divisions of the British and American armies had entered the area around Aachen. Our remaining U-boats sent word that they had sunk three freighters in the Irish Sea, but along the Rhine front, pressure on Colmar was growing. In the Balkans, the partisans around Sarajevo were becoming more aggressive. The 2nd Mountain Troop Division was withdrawn from Jylland in Denmark to reinforce sections of the eastern front. In Budapest, where supply problems were worsening from day to day, the front ran directly below the castle. Everywhere dead bodies were left behind, on both sides. Identification tags were collected, decorations handed out.

What else happened, aside from the fact that promised miracle weapons failed to appear? In Silesia, attacks near Glogau were repulsed, but around Posen the fighting intensified. And near Kulm, Soviet units crossed the Vistula. In East Prussia the enemy advanced to Bartenstein and Bischofswerder. Up to this day, which was nothing special in itself, the authorities had managed to get sixty-five thousand people, civilian and military, onto boats in Pillau. Everywhere monument-worthy heroic deeds were performed; others were in the offing. As the *Wilhelm Gustloff* on its westward course was approaching the Stolpe Bank, and the submarine *S-13* was still prowling for prey, eleven hundred four-engine enemy bombers conducted a night raid on the area around Hamm, Bielefeld, and Kassel, and the American president had already left the United States; Roosevelt was on his way to Yalta, the conference site on the Crimean peninsula, where the ailing man would meet with Churchill and Stalin to pave the way for peace by drawing new borders.

On the subject of this conference and the subsequent one in Potsdam, which took place when Roosevelt was dead and Truman president, I found hate pages on the Internet and a sort of throwaway comment on my know-it-all son's Web site: "This is how they dismembered our Germany," along with a map of the Greater German Reich, with all the lost territories marked. He then speculated on the miracles that might have occurred if the young sailors, almost finished with their training, had safely reached their destination of Kiel on the *Gustloff* and been successfully deployed, manning twelve or more U-boats of the new, fabulously fast and almost silent XXIII Class. His wish list bristled with heroic deeds and special victory announcements. Konny didn't go quite so far as to invoke the final victory retroactively, but he was sure that these young U-boatmen would have experienced a better death, even if these miracle vessels had been destroyed by depth charges, than proved their lot when they drowned wretchedly opposite the Stolpe Bank. His opponent David agreed with the comparative weight assigned to these ways of death, but then tossed some reservations into the Net: "Those young fellows really had no choice. No matter what, they had no chance of surviving to adulthood..."

Photos are available, collected over decades by the purser's assistant after he survived the disaster: many small passport-sized ones and a group photo showing all the sailors who would normally have undergone four months of training with the 2nd Submarine Training Division. They are lined up on the sundeck, having saluted Lieutenant Commander Zahn and now, after the command "At ease!," standing there in a more relaxed posture. On this wide-angle photograph, showing over nine hundred sailor hats, which get smaller and smaller toward the stern, individual faces can be made out only as far back as the seventh row. Behind that an orderly mass. But from the passport-sized photos, one uniformed man after another gazes out at me. These youthful faces, although they may all be different, have the same unfinished quality. They must be about eighteen. Some boys, photographed in uniform during the final months of the war, are even younger. My son, seventeen by now, could be one of them, although, because of his glasses, Konny would hardly have qualified for submarine duty.

They are all wearing their admittedly becoming sailor caps, with the band that reads GERMAN NAVY at a cocky angle, usually tilted toward the right. I see round, narrow, angular, and chubby-cheeked faces on these death candidates. Their uniform is their pride and joy. They gaze out at me, their solemnity prophetically appropriate for this last photograph.

The few photos available to me of the 375 girls of the naval auxiliary make a more civilian impression, in spite of their little two-pointed service caps, also worn at an angle, with the imperial eagle bent around the point at the front. The young girls' neat hairdos—many no doubt achieved by means of permanent or water waves— fall in the curls fashionable at the time. Quite a few of the girls may have been engaged, only a few married. Two or three, who make a coolly sensuous impression on me with their straight hair, remind me of my ex-wife. That is how Gabi looked back in the day when she was a fairly dedicated education student in Berlin and made my heart drop to my knees the moment I saw her. At first glance almost all the naval auxiliaries are pretty, even cute; some of them show early signs of a double chin. They have a less solemn expression than the boys. Each one gazing out at me smiles unsuspectingly.

Because not even a hundred survived of the far more than four thousand infants, children, and youths aboard the doomed ship, only a few photos turned up; the refugees' baggage, with family photo albums from East and West Prussia, Danzig, and Gotenhafen, went down with the ship. I see the children's faces from those years. Girls with braids and bows, the boys with hair slicked down, parted on the left or right. There are hardly any pictures of infants, who in any case have a timeless appearance. The photographs of mothers who found their grave in the Baltic and of the few who remained alive, mostly without their children, were "snapped" (as Mother would say) either long before the disaster or many years later on family occasions; of Mother there is not a single photo from that era—or of me as a baby.

By the same token, no likeness remains of those old men and women—Masurian peasants, retired civil servants, merry widows, and tradesmen—the thousands of elderly people, distraught from the horrors of their flight, who were allowed on board. All men in their middle years were turned back on the Oxhöft dock because they were eligible for the last Landsturm call-ups. Among those saved from going down with the ship, thus, were hardly any men or women of advanced years. And no picture preserves the memory of the wounded soldiers from the Kurland who lay packed onto cots in the Bower.

The few older people who were rescued included the ship's captain, Petersen, a man in his mid-sixties. At nine o'clock in the evening all four captains were standing on the bridge, arguing over whether it had been right to carry out Petersen's order and set running lights, an order given merely because shortly after six that evening a convoy of minesweepers had been reported by radio to be approaching in the opposite direction. Zahn had opposed the move. The second navigation captain likewise. Petersen did allow some of the lights to be turned off, but kept the port and starboard lights on. With only the torpedo boat *Löwe* serving as an escort, and with no lights indicating its height or length, the darkened ship continued on course through diminishing snowfall and heavy swell, approaching the Stolpe Bank, marked on all nautical maps. The predicted moderate frost registered −18° Celsius.

We are told that it was the first officer of the Soviet U-boat *S-13* who spotted running lights in the distance. Whoever reported the sighting, Marinesko promptly made his way to the tower, as the submarine moved along above water. Apparently he was wearing, along with his fur-trimmed cap, or *ushanka,* not the lined coat that was standard issue for U-boat officers but instead an oil-smeared sheepskin slung over his shoulders.

During the boat's long underwater cruise, which was powered by its electric engines, the captain had received reports only of sounds from small ships. Near Hela he had given the order to surface. The diesel engines came on. Only now did a ship with twin propellers become audible. Heavy snow that set in suddenly protected the submarine, but reduced visibility. As the snow subsided, the outlines of a troop transport, estimated at twenty thousand tons, and an escort vessel came into view. The submarine was on the ocean side, looking toward the transport's starboard side and the Pomeranian coastline, whose presence could be dimly sensed. For the time being nothing happened.

I can only speculate as to what induced the captain of *S-13* to increase the boat's speed and, still above the surface, circle the ship and its escort from behind and then try to find an attack position on the coastal side, in water less than thirty meters deep. According to later explanations, he was determined to strike, wherever he could find them, the "fascist dogs" who had treacherously attacked his fatherland and devastated it; up to now he had not had much luck.

For two weeks his search for prey had yielded nothing. He had not got off a single shot, either near the island of Gotland or in the Baltic harbors of Windau and Memel. Not one of the ten torpedoes on board had left its tube. Marinesko must have been starved for action. Besides, this man whose competence manifested itself only at sea must have been haunted by the fear that if he returned empty-handed to port in Turku or Hangö, he would be immediately hauled before the court-martial that the NKVD had called for. The charges were not limited to his most recent drinking bout and the overstayed shore leave he had spent in Finnish whorehouses; he was also under suspicion of espionage, an accusation common in the Soviet Union since the mid-thirties as the pretext for purges, and impossible to refute. All that could save him was an incontrovertible success.

After almost two hours on the surface, the U-boat had accomplished its circumnavigation maneuver. *S-13* was now sailing parallel to the enemy vessel, which to the astonishment of the tower crew had running lights lit and was not tacking. Since it had completely stopped snowing, there was a risk that the clouds might part, leaving not only the huge transport and its escort ship exposed in the moonlight but also the U-boat.

Marinesko nonetheless adhered to his decision to launch an above-water attack. An advantage for *S-13*, which no one on the submarine could have guessed, was that the U-boat locater on the torpedo boat *Löwe* was frozen and unable to pick up any echoes. In their account, the English authors Dobson, Miller, and Payne assume that the Soviet commander had been practicing surface attacks for a long time because German submarines had had great success with this method in the Atlantic, and now he wanted a chance to try it out. An above-water attack provides better visibility, as well as greater speed and precision.

Marinesko now gave an order to reduce buoyancy until the body of the boat was underwater, leaving only the tower poking out of the choppy sea. Allegedly a signal flare was seen coming from the bridge of the target vessel shortly before the attack, and light signals were spotted; but none of the German sources—the accounts of the surviving captains—confirm this report.

Thus *S-13* approached the port side of the target vessel unimpeded. On instructions from the commander, the four torpedoes in the bow were set to strike at three meters below the surface. The estimated distance to the target was six hundred meters. The periscope had the ship's bow in its crosshairs. It was 2304 hours Moscow Time, precisely two hours earlier German Time.

But before Marinesko's order to fire is issued and can no longer be retracted, I must insert into this report a legend that has been passed down. Before *S-13* left Hangö Harbor, a crew member by the name of Pichur allegedly took a brush and painted dedications on all the torpedoes, including the four that were now ready to be fired. The first read FOR THE MOTHERLAND, the torpedo in tube 2 was marked FOR STALIN, and in tubes 3 and 4 the dedications painted onto the eel-smooth surfaces read FOR THE SOVIET PEOPLE and FOR LENINGRAD.

Their significance thus predetermined, when the order was finally issued, three of the four torpedoes—the one dedicated to Stalin stuck in its tube and had to be hastily disarmed—zoomed toward the ship, nameless from Marinesko's point of view, in whose maternity ward Mother was still asleep, lulled by soft music on the radio.

While the three inscribed torpedoes are speeding toward their target, I am tempted to think my way aboard the *Gustloff.* I have no trouble finding the last group of naval auxiliary girls to embark, who were billeted in the drained swimming pool, also in the adjacent youth hostel area, used originally for members of the Hitler Youth and League of German Girls when they were sent on holiday cruises. The girls sit and lie there, packed in tightly. Their hairdos are still in place. But no more laughter, no more easygoing or sharp-tongued gossip. Some of the girls are seasick. There and throughout the corridors of the other decks, in the former reception rooms and dining rooms, is the smell of vomit. The toilets, in any case far too few for the mass of refugees and navy personnel, are stopped up. The ventilation system is not powerful enough to draw off the stench along with the stale air. Since the ship got under way, all the passengers have had orders to wear the life jackets that were handed out earlier, but because of the increasing heat many people are stripping off their warm underwear and also their life jackets. Old folks and children are whining plaintively. No more announcements over the public address system. All sounds subdued. Resigned sighing and whimpering. What I picture is not a sense of impending doom but its precursor: fear creeping in.

Only on the bridge, with the worst of the conflict resolved, was the mood reportedly somewhat optimistic. The four captains thought that having reached the Stolpe Bank, they had put the greatest danger behind them. In the first officer's cabin a meal was being consumed: pea soup with ham. Afterward, Lieutenant Commander Zahn had the steward pour a round of cognac. It seemed appropriate to drink to a voyage on which Fortune was smiling. At his master's feet slept the German shepherd Hassan. Only Captain Weller was on watch on the bridge. Meanwhile time had run out.

From childhood on, I have heard Mother's often repeated formulation: "The first time it went boom I was
wide awake, and then it came again, and again..."

The first torpedo hit the bow of the ship far below the
waterline, in the area where the crew quarters lay. Any
crew member who was off watch, munching a hunk of
bread or sleeping in his bunk, and survived the explo-
sion, nonetheless did not escape, because after the first
report of damage Captain Weller ordered the automatic
closing of the watertight doors, sealing off the forward
part of the ship, to prevent the vessel from sinking rapidly at the bow; an emergency drill in closing the watertight doors had been conducted just before the ship put
out to sea. Among the sailors and Croatian volunteers
thus sacrificed were many who had been drilled in load-
ing and lowering the lifeboats in an orderly fashion.

What took place—suddenly, gradually, finally—in
the closed-off forward portion of the ship no one knows.

Mother's next utterance also made an indelible impression: "At the second boom I fell out of bed, that's
how bad it was..." This torpedo from tube 3, whose
smooth surface carried the inscription FOR THE SOVIET
PEOPLE," exploded beneath the swimming pool on E deck.
Only two or three girls from the naval auxiliary survived. Later they spoke of smelling gas, and of seeing
girls cut to pieces by glass shards from the mosaic that
had adorned the front wall of the pool area and by splin-
tered tiles from the pool itself. As the water rushed in,
one could see corpses and body parts floating in it, along
with sandwiches and other remains of supper, also

empty life jackets. Hardly any screaming. Then the light went out. These two or three naval auxiliaries, of whom I have no passport-sized photos, managed to escape through an emergency exit, behind which a companion-way led steeply up to the higher decks.

And then Mother said, "Not till the third boom" had Dr. Richter turned up to check on the women in the maternity ward. "By that time all hell'd broke loose!" she exclaimed every time her neverending story reached "number 3."

The last torpedo hit the engine room amidships, knocking out not only the engines but also the interior lighting on all decks, as well as the ship's other systems. After that everything took place in darkness. Only the emergency lighting that came on a few minutes later provided some sense of orientation amid the chaos, as panic broke out everywhere on the two-hundred-meter-long and ten-story-high ship, which could no longer send out an SOS; the equipment in the radio room had also gone dead. Only from the torpedo boat *Löwe* did the repeated call go out into the ether: "*Gustloff* sinking after three torpedo strikes!" In between, the location of the sinking ship was transmitted over and over, for hours: "Position Stolpmünde, 55.07 degrees north, 17.42 degrees east. Request assistance..."

On *S-13,* the successful hits and the soon unmistakable sinking of the target gave rise to quiet rejoicing. Captain Marinesko issued an order for the partially pre-flooded submarine to submerge, because he knew that this close to the coast, and especially over the Stolpe

Bank, there was little protection from depth charges. First the torpedo stuck in tube 2 had to be disarmed; if it remained sitting there, ready for ignition, with the firing motor running, the slightest vibration could cause it to explode. Fortunately no depth charges were dropped. The torpedo boat *Löwe,* its engines cut, was sweeping the mortally wounded ship with its searchlights.

On our global playground, the vaunted ultimate venue for communication, the Soviet U-boat *S-13* was labeled categorically "the murder vessel," this on the Web site to which I had a familial connection. The crew of this naval unit belonging to the Baltic Red Banner Fleet were condemned as "murderers of women and children." On the Internet my son set himself up as the judge. When his bosom enemy raised objections—all he could think of was cranking up his antifascist prayer wheel and calling attention to the high-ranking Nazis and military personnel on board, and the 3-cm antiaircraft guns mounted on the sundeck—they were no match for the comments that now flooded in from all continents. Most of the chatters chimed in in German, with scraps of English. The usual hate stuff, but also pious invocations of the apocalypse, filled my screen. Exclamation points following the balance of terror. Here and there casualty figures from other maritime disasters for purposes of comparison.

The frequently filmed drama of the *Titanic* was trying to maintain its lead. Close behind came the *Lusitania,* sunk during the First World War by a German U-boat, which supposedly led to the USA's entry into the war, or at least hastened it. A lone voice also piped up with the sinking of the *Cap Arcona,* loaded with concentration-camp inmates, by English bombers in the Bay of Neustadt in Holstein; this mistake occurred only a few days before the end of the war, and for now topped the charts on the Internet, with seven thousand dead. Then the *Goya* climbed to the same level. But in the end the *Gustloff* won out in this competitive numerical chatter. With the zeal fueled by his passion for thoroughness, my son had succeeded in using his Web site to draw the right wing circles' muddled attention to the forgotten ship and its human cargo, rendering the vessel visible in the form of a schematic drawing, with jagged-edged circles marking the spots where the torpedoes had hit, so that from then on the ship's name came to carry global significance as the epitome of disaster.

But the statistics fighting it out in cyberspace had little to do with what actually took place on the *Wilhelm Gustloff,* starting at 2116 hours on 30 January 1945. In spite of the overly drawn-out prologue, Frank Wisbar did a better job of capturing, in his black-and-white film *Night Fell over Gotenhafen,* something of the panic that erupted on all decks when the three hits caused the ship to heel to port, with the bow already under water from the first hit.

Past omissions came home to roost. Why hadn't the lifeboats, of which there were too few in any case, been swung out in anticipation of being needed? Why hadn't the davits and block and tackle been deiced at regular intervals? In addition, there was the absence of the crew members trapped in the forward part of the ship when the watertight doors were closed—and perhaps even still alive. The naval recruits from the training division had no experience with lifeboats. The mass of people crowding from the upper decks onto the slick, ice-coated sundeck, which was also the boat deck, slipped and slid as the boat listed. Already the first ones went flying overboard, because there was nothing to hang on to. Not all of those who fell wore life jackets. Now many jumped into the water out of sheer panic. Because of the heat inside the ship, most of those making their way onto the sundeck were too lightly dressed to withstand the shock of an air temperature of $-18°$ Celsius and correspondingly low water temperature—was it two or three degrees warmer? Even so they jumped.

From the bridge came orders to steer all those pushing toward the boat deck into the glass-enclosed lower promenade deck, to shut the doors and post armed guards, in the hope that rescue ships would arrive. The order was strictly enforced. This glass case measuring 165 meters and stretching from port to starboard imprisoned a thousand people or more. Not until the very end, when it was too late, did some sections of the promenade deck's plate glass shatter from the pressure.

But what took place inside the ship cannot be captured in words. Mother's phrase for anything indescribable—"There's no notes in the scale for it..."—expresses what I dimly mean. So I won't even try to imagine those terrible sights and to force the gruesome scene into painstakingly depicted images, no matter how my employer is pressuring me to present a series of individual fates, to convey the entire situation with sweeping narrative equanimity and the utmost empathy and thus, with words of horror, do justice to the full extent of the catastrophe.

Such an attempt was undertaken by that black-and-white film, with images shot in a studio. You see masses of people pushing, clogged corridors, the struggle for every step up the staircase; you see costumed extras imprisoned in the closed promenade deck, feel the ship listing, see the water rising, see people swimming inside the ship, see people drowning. And you see children in the film. Children separated from their mothers. Children holding dangling dolls. Children wandering lost along corridors that have already been vacated. Close-ups of the eyes of individual children. But the more than four thousand infants, children, and youths for whom no survival was possible were not filmed, simply for reasons of expense; they remained, and will remain, an abstract number, like all the other numbers in the thousands, hundred thousands, millions, that then as now could only be estimated. One zero more or less—what does it matter? In statistics, what disappears behind rows of numbers is death.

I can only report what has been quoted elsewhere from the testimony of survivors. On broad staircases and narrow companionways old people and children were trampled to death. It was every man for himself. The more considerate among them tried to steal a march on death. Thus one training officer is said to have gathered

his family in the cabin assigned to them, where he shot
first his three children, then his wife, and finally himself
with his service revolver. Similar stories are told of promi-
nent Party members and their families, who put an end
to their lives in those very luxury staterooms built for
Hitler and his vassal Ley and now providing the setting
for self-activated liquidation. It may be assumed that
Hassan, the lieutenant commander's dog, was likewise
shot, by his master. On the ice-coated sundeck, weapons
also had to be used, because the order "Only women and
children to the boats" was not being observed, with the
end result that primarily men survived, as the statistics
proved, those statistics that wrap up life soberly and
without commentary.

A boat that could have accommodated fifty was
lowered into the water prematurely, with only about a
dozen sailors in it. Another boat, having been let down
too hastily and still attached by the cable in front, tipped
all its passengers into the choppy sea and then, when the
cable snapped, fell on top of those who were floundering
in the water. Reportedly only lifeboat 4, half occupied by
women and children, was lowered correctly. Since the
critically wounded soldiers in the emergency ward set
up in the Bower were doomed in any case, medics tried
to get some of the less seriously wounded into the boats:
in vain.

Even those in charge thought only of themselves.
There is a report of a high-ranking officer who fetched
his wife from their cabin on the upper deck and began to
deice the mountings of a motor launch that had been used

in KDF times as an excursion boat during trips to Norway. When he finally succeeded in swinging the motor boat out, wonder of wonders, the electric windlass was working. As the launch was being lowered from the boat deck, the women and children imprisoned in the enclosed promenade deck saw it through the plate-glass panels, only half occupied; and the occupants of the launch caught sight for a moment of the mass of humanity crammed in behind the glass. The two groups could have waved to each other. The rest of what happened inside the ship remained unseen, never to be put into words.

All I know is how Mother was rescued. "Right after that last boom, the labor pains started..." As a child, when I heard her begin that way, I thought I was in for a thrilling adventure story, but she soon punctured the expectation: "And then the nice doctor quickly gave me a shot..." She had been scared of the "prick," "but that stopped the pains..."

It must have been Dr. Richter who saw to it that two new mothers with their infants and Mother were helped across the slippery sundeck by the head nurse and seated in a boat that had already been swung out of its berth and was suspended in its davits. With another pregnant woman and one who had suffered a miscarriage, the doctor reportedly soon afterward found a spot in one of the last boats—apparently without Nurse Helga.

Mother told me that as the ship listed more sharply, one of the 3-cm antiaircraft guns on the afterdeck broke free from its mounting, plummeted overboard, and smashed a fully occupied lifeboat that had just been lowered. "That was right next to us. Just goes to show how lucky we were..."

So I left the sinking ship in Mother's womb. Our boat cast off, and, surrounded by drifting bodies, some still alive, others already dead, put some distance between itself and the listing port side of the ship, from which I would like to extract another story or two before it's too late. For instance, the one about the popular ship's hairdresser, who for years had been collecting the increasingly rare silver five-mark pieces. Now he leaped into the sea with a bulging pouch on his belt, and the weight of the silver promptly... But I'm not allowed to tell any more stories.

I am advised to cut it short, no, my employer insists. Since I'm not managing in any case, he says, to capture the thousandfold dying in the belly of the boat and in the icy water, to perform a German requiem or a maritime *danse macabre,* I should leave well enough alone, get to the point. He means my birth.

But the moment has not yet come. In the boat in which Mother was seated, without parents or luggage, but with postponed contractions, all the occupants had a clear view from an increasing distance, and whenever a wave lifted them, of the *Wilhelm Gustloff,* sinking at a catastrophically steep angle. As the searchlight of the escort vessel, which was holding its position to one side in heavy seas, kept raking the bridge superstructure, the glassed-in promenade deck, and the sundeck, tilted sharply up to starboard, those who had managed to escape into the boat witnessed individuals and clumps of people hurtling overboard. And close by, Mother, and all those who wanted to see, saw people drifting in their life jackets, some still alive and calling out loudly or feebly for help, pleading to be taken into the lifeboats, and others, already dead, who looked as if they were asleep. But even worse, Mother said, was the fate of the children: "They all skidded off the ship the wrong way round, headfirst. So there they was, floating in them bulky life jackets, their little legs poking up in the air..."

Later, when Mother was asked by the journeymen in her carpenters' brigade or by the man with whom she was sleeping at the moment, how she had come to have white hair at such a young age, she would say, "It happened when I saw all them little children, head down in the water..."

It's possible that this really was when the shock first took effect. When I was a child and mother was in her mid-twenties, she displayed her cropped white hair like a trophy. Whenever someone asked, it brought up a subject that was not allowed in the Workers' and Peasants' State: the *Gustloff* and its sinking. But sometimes, with cautious casualness, she would also talk about the Soviet U-boat and the three torpedoes; she always employed stilted High German when she referred to the commander of *S-13* and his men as "the heroes of the Soviet Union allied to us workers in friendship."

Around the time when, according to Mother's testimony, her hair suddenly turned white—probably a good half hour after the torpedoes struck their target—the crew of the submerged submarine were keeping still, expecting depth charges, which, however, did not come. No sound of an approaching ship's propeller. None of the drama one associates with scenes in U-boat films. But Petty Officer Shnapzev, whose assignment was to pick up external noises in his earphones, heard the sounds from the body of the sinking ship: rumbling, caused when engine blocks broke free from their mountings, a loud popping when, after a brief creaking, the watertight doors snapped under the water pressure, and other indefinable noises. All this he reported to his commander in an undertone.

Since in the meantime the torpedo stuck in tube 2 and dedicated to Stalin had been disarmed, and the order for absolute silence in the boat was still in force, the petty officer with the earphones could pick up, in addition to the sounds that made the dying and still anonymous ship audible to him, the distant noise of the escort vessel, moving slowly. No danger emanated from there. Human voices he did not hear.

It was the torpedo boat, still holding its position with engines throttled, from whose railing ropes were lowered to fish the living and the dead out of the water. Since its only motorized dinghy was iced up, besides which the motor refused to start, it could not be used to help with the rescue effort. Ropes were the only devices available. About two hundred survivors came on board in this fashion.

When the first of the few lifeboats that could get free of the hesitantly capsizing ship headed for the *Löwe* and came alongside in the light cone of its searchlight, they had trouble docking in the choppy sea. Mother, who was in one of the boats, said, "First a wave would lift us high up, so we was looking down on the *Löwe,* then we'd be in the cellar, with the *Löwe* way above over us..."

Only when the lifeboat hovered at the level of the torpedo boat's railing—which meant for seconds at a time—did it prove possible to transfer individual survivors to safety. Anyone who missed the jump fell between the boats and was lost. But with luck Mother landed aboard a warship with only 768 tons of displacement, launched in '38 from a Norwegian wharf, christened the *Gyller,* placed in Norwegian service, and seized by the German navy when Norway was occupied in '40.

Two sailors from the escort ship with this prehistory hoisted Mother over the railing. She lost her shoes in the process, and they had hardly wrapped her in a blanket and taken her to the cabin of the engineer on duty when the contractions resumed.

Make a wish! It's not that I want to introduce a distraction, which a certain someone might impute to me; but instead of being born to Mother on the *Löwe,* I wish I could have been that foundling rescued by the patrol boat *VP-1703* seven hours after the ship went down. That happened after additional ships, chief among them the torpedo boat *T-36,* then the steamers *Gotenland* and *Göttingen,* had plucked the few survivors from the swell amid ice porridge, ice floes, and many lifeless bodies.

In Gotenhafen, the SOS calls broadcast repeatedly by the *Löwe*'s radio operator were reported to the captain of the patrol boat. He immediately set out in his rust bucket, and came upon a sea of corpses. Nonetheless he repeatedly scanned the sea with the onboard searchlight, until the cone of light picked up a lifeboat that was drifting as if unmanned. Chief Botswain Fick climbed down into the boat and found, next to the stiffened corpses of a woman and a half-grown girl, a frozen bundle wrapped in a wool blanket, which, when brought aboard *VP-1703* and freed of the outer coating of ice, was unrolled, bringing to light that infant I would like to have been: a foundling without parents, the last survivor of the *Wilhelm Gustloff.*

The fleet doctor, who happened to be on duty on the patrol boat that night, felt the infant's weak pulse, started resuscitation efforts, ventured to administer a camphor injection, and did not rest until the child, a boy, opened his eyes. The doctor estimated his age at eleven months, and set up a provisional document in which he recorded all the important details—the lack of a name, the unknown origin, the approximate age, the day and hour of the rescue, and the name and rank of the rescuer.

That would have suited me: to have been born not on that ill-starred 30 January but at the end of February or the beginning of March '44 in some East Prussian hamlet, on an unknown day, to Mother Unknown, begotten

by Father Nowheretobefound, but adopted by my rescuer, Chief Botswain Werner Fick, who would have
placed me in the care of his wife at the first opportunity—
in Swinemünde. When the war ended, I would have
moved with my adoptive, otherwise childless parents to
the bombed-out city of Hamburg in the British zone.
But a year later, in Fick's hometown of Rostock, located
in the Soviet occupation zone and likewise bombed out,
we would have found a place to live. From then on, I
would have grown up parallel to my actual biography,
in which I am tethered to Mother, would have partici-
pated in the same things—the Young Pioneers' flag waving, the Free German Youth parades—but cherished by
the Ficks. That I would have enjoyed. Pampered by father and mother, as a foundling whose diaper revealed
nothing about his origins, I would have grown up in
a concrete-slab apartment complex, would have been
called Peter, not Paul, would have studied shipbuilding
and been hired by the Neptune Shipyards in Rostock,
holding a secure job up to the fall of the Wall, and would
have been present at the reunion of survivors in the Baltic
sea resort of Damp, fifty years after my rescue, an early
retiree, alone or with my now elderly adoptive parents,
celebrated by all the participants, pointed out on the
stage: he was that foundling.

Someone—maybe that damned destiny, for all I
care—didn't want that for me. I had no escape route.
Was not permitted to survive as a nameless found object.
When the lifeboat was in the right position, Fräulein
Ursula Pokriefke, as she was listed in the boat's log, in an

advanced state of pregnancy, was transferred to the *Löwe*. Even the time was noted: 2205 hours. While death's harvest continued to reap rich gains in the churned-up sea and inside the *Gustloff,* nothing more stood in the way of Mother's delivery.

This much must be conceded: my birth was not unique. The aria "Snatch life from the jaws of death" had several verses. Children came into the world before me and after me that day. On torpedo boat *T-36,* as well as on the *Göttingen,* a six-thousand-ton steamer of the North German Lloyd Line, which arrived somewhat later, having taken on board in the East Prussia harbor of Pillau two and a half thousand wounded and more than a thousand refugees, among them almost a hundred infants. During the voyage, five more children were born, the last shortly before the ship, traveling in a convoy, reached the sea of corpses, hardly enlivened anymore by cries for help. But at the actual moment when the *Gustloff* went down, sixty-two minutes after the torpedoes struck, I was the only one to crawl out of my hole.

"At the exact minute when the *Yustloff* went under," Mother asserts or, as I would describe it: when the *Wilhelm Gustloff,* bow first and listing sharply, at the same time sank and capsized to the port side, which meant that all the people slithering down the upper decks, also the stacks of rafts, indeed everything that wasn't nailed down, hurtled into the foaming sea; at the moment when, as if on orders from the back of beyond, the ship's lighting, extinguished since the torpedoes hit, suddenly came on inside and even on the decks, and—as in peacetime and the KDF years—offered all who had eyes to see one last spectacle of festive illumination; at the moment when everything came to an end, I was born, so they tell me, quite normally, in the engineer's narrow bunk bed: headfirst and without complications, or, as Mother said, "It went without a hitch. You just popped out..."

She missed everything taking place outside that bunk bed. She saw neither the festive illumination of the capsizing ship as it went under nor the tangled bunches of people plummeting from the stern, the last part to remain above water. But as Mother claims to remember, my first cry drowned out that other cry, blended from thousands of voices and carrying far and wide over the water, that final cry that came from everywhere: from the interior of the collapsing ship, from the bursting promenade deck, from the flooded sundeck, from the rapidly vanishing stern, and rising from the turbulent surface of the water, where thousands swirled, dead or alive, in their life jackets. From half-filled or overcrowded boats, from densely packed rafts, which were swept aloft on the crests of the waves, then disappeared into the troughs, from everywhere the cry rose into the air, escalating to a gruesome duet with the ship's siren, which suddenly began to wail, and just as suddenly was choked off. A collective death cry such as had never before been heard, of which Mother said, and will continue to say, "A cry like that—you won't ever get it out of your ear..."

The ensuing silence was disturbed only by my whimpering, or so I hear. Once the umbilical cord was cut, I too fell silent. When the captain, as witness to the sinking, had noted the exact time in his ship's log, the crew of the torpedo boat went back to fishing survivors out of the sea.

But that's not how it was. Mother is lying. I'm certain that it wasn't on the *Löwe* that I... The time was actually... Because when the second torpedo... And at the first contractions, Dr. Richter... not an injection but actually delivered... Went smoothly. Born on a slanting, sliding cot. Everything was slanting when I... Only a pity that Dr. Richter didn't have time to fill out the form, by hand: born on... on board the... at... No, no, not on a torpedo boat but on board that damned ship, named after the martyr, launched in Hamburg, once gleaming white, much loved, promoting strength through joy, classless, thrice-cursed, overcrowded, battleship-gray, torpedoed, everlastingly sinking: that's where I was born, headfirst and on a slant. Once the umbilical cord was cut, and I was diapered and swaddled in one of the ship's wool blankets, Mother and I were helped into the lifesaving boat by Dr. Richter and Head Nurse Helga.

But she doesn't want a delivery on the *Gustloff*. Cooks up two sailors who cut my umbilical cord in the chief engineer's cabin. In another version it is the doctor, who, however, was not yet on the torpedo boat at that time. Even Mother, otherwise always absolutely sure of herself, wavers in her account, and sometimes, in addition to "them two seamen" and "the nice doctor who gave me a shot while I was still on the *Yustloff*," places another person at the scene of the delivery: the captain of the *Löwe*, Paul Prüfe, is supposed to have cut my umbilical cord.

Since I have no way to corroborate my version of the birth, which admittedly is more like a vision, I shall stick to the facts as reported by Heinz Schön; according to him, Dr. Richter was taken aboard the *Löwe* sometime after midnight. Only then did he preside over the birth of some other child. Beyond a doubt, it was the *Gustloff*'s doctor who later filled out my birth certificate, giving the date of 30 January 1945, although without an exact time. It was Lieutenant Commander Prüfe, however, who was responsible for my given name. Mother is said to have insisted that I be called Paul, "just like the captain of the *Löwe*," and there was no choice as to my last name, Pokriefke. Later the boys in school and in the Free German Youth, but also fellow journalists, called me "Peepee," and I sign my articles P dot P dot.

By the way, the boy born on the torpedo boat two hours after me, which means on 31 January, was called Leo, at his mother's request and in honor of the ship that had rescued her.

There were no arguments on the Internet about any of this—my birth and the people who supposedly played a role in it, on one ship or the other; my son's Web site made no mention of a Paul Pokriefke, not even in abbreviated form. Absolute silence about anything having to do with me. My son simply left me out. I didn't exist online. But another ship, which, accompanied by the torpedo boat *T-36,* arrived at the site of the catastrophe at the moment of the sinking or a few minutes later, the heavy cruiser *Admiral Hipper,* unleashed a quarrel between Konrad and his nemesis David, a quarrel that would later unravel across the globe.

Fact is, the *Hipper,* likewise overloaded with refugees and wounded, paused only briefly, but then turned away to continue on course to Kiel. While Konny, portraying himself as an expert on maritime questions, assessed the warning about submarines in the area as sufficient grounds for the heavy cruiser's turning away, David objected that the *Hipper* should have at least lowered some of its motor launches and made them available for further rescue operations. Furthermore, when the warship, with its ten thousand tons of displacement, executed its turning maneuver at full power in the immediate vicinity of the disaster site, a large number of people floating in the water were sucked into the boat's wake; not a few were shredded by the propellers.

My son, however, claimed to know for a fact that the *Hipper*'s escort vessel had not only picked up U-boat presence on its locater, *T-36* had actually managed to evade two torpedoes aimed at it. In response, David described, as if he had been there underwater, how the successful Soviet U-boat had kept motionless, not raising its periscope and not firing a single torpedo, while the detonation of the depth charges dropped by *T-36* blew to bits many people drifting in life jackets and calling for help. As an epilogue to the tragedy, he claimed, a massacre had occurred.

Now there ensued the kind of no-holds-barred total communication possible on the Internet. Voices from home and abroad joined in. One contribution even came from Alaska. You could see how current the sinking of the long-forgotten ship had become. With the exclamation, seemingly emanating from the present, "The *Gustloff* is sinking!," my son's home page opened a window to the entire world, launching what even David conceded online was "a much overdue discourse." Yes, of course! Now everyone could know and judge for himself what had happened on 30 January 1945 off the Stolpe Bank; the Webmaster had scanned in a map of the Baltic and marked with didactic precision all the sea-lanes leading to the site of the tragedy.

Unfortunately Konny's adversary did not refrain, toward the end of the globally expanding chatter, from bringing up the further significance of that fatal date and reminding everyone of the man for whom the sunken ship was named, portraying the murder of the party functionary Wilhelm Gustloff by the medical student David Frankfurter as "on the one hand regrettable for the widow, on the other hand—in consideration of the Jewish people's suffering—a necessary and farsighted act." He even began to celebrate the sinking of the huge ship by a small U-boat as a continuation of the "eternal struggle of David against Goliath." His pathos escalated; he tossed expressions like "hereditary guilt" and "obligation to atone" into the networked ether. He praised the commandant of *S-13* for his sure aim, calling him a worthy successor to the sure-aimed medical student: "Marinesko's courage and Frankfurter's heroic act should never be forgotten!"

The chat room promptly filled with hate. "Jewish scum" and "Auschwitz liar" were the mildest insults. As the sinking of the ship was dredged up for a new generation, the long-submerged hate slogan "Death to all Jews" bubbled to the digital surface of contemporary reality: foaming hate, a maelstrom of hate. Good God! How much of this has been dammed up all this time, is growing day by day, building pressure for action.

My son, however, showed restraint. His tone was quite polite when he inquired, "So tell me, David, is it possible that you're of Jewish descent?" The response was ambiguous: "My dear Wilhelm, if it will give you pleasure or help you in some other way, you can send me to the gas chamber the next time an occasion arises."

7

THE DEVIL ONLY KNOWS WHO KNOCKED MOTHER up. Sometimes it's supposed to have been her cousin, in the dark woodshed on Elsenstrasse in Langfuhr; sometimes it was a Luftwaffe auxiliary from the antiaircraft battery near the Kaiserhafen—"in sight of the pile o' bones"—then a sergeant who allegedly gnashed his teeth as he ejaculated. It doesn't matter; whoever it was who fucked her, to me her random finger-pointing meant only this: born and raised without a father, doomed to become a father myself someday.

Still, a certain someone, who is about Mother's age and claims to have known her only casually, as Tulla, patronizingly gives me permission to explain my screwed-up existence in a few words. He is of the opinion that my failure with my son speaks for itself, but if I absolutely insist, the trauma of my birth can be cited as a possible extenuating factor for my ineptitude as a father. Still, all private conjectures aside, the actual events will have to remain in the foreground.

Thanks a lot! I can manage without explanations. I've always found absolute judgments repellent. Only this much: your humble servant's existence is purely a matter of chance, for as I was born in Captain Prüfe's cabin and mingled my cry with the cry that for Mother refused to end, three frozen infants were lying under a sheet in the next bunk. Later others were added, they say: ice-blue.

After the heavy cruiser *Hipper,* with its ten thousand tons of displacement, had shredded dead bodies, and some that were still alive, as it executed its turning maneuver, and then sucked them under, the search was resumed. Little by little other boats arrived to aid the two torpedo boats. In addition to the steamers, that included several minesweepers and a torpedo interceptor, and finally *VP-1703,* which rescued the foundling.

After that, there were no more signs of life. Only corpses were fished out of the water. The children, their legs poking into the air. At last the sea above the mass grave was calm.

The numbers I am about to mention are not accurate. Everything will always be approximate. Besides, numbers don't say much. The ones with lots of zeros can't be grasped. It's in their nature to contradict each other. Not only did the total number of people on board the *Gustloff* remain uncertain for many decades—it was somewhere between 6,600 and 10,600—but the number of survivors also had to be corrected repeatedly: starting with 900 and finally set at 1,230. This raises the question, to which no answer can be hoped for: What does one life more or less count?

We do know that the majority of those who died were women and children; men were rescued in embarrassingly large numbers, among them all four captains of the ship. Petersen, who died shortly after the end of the war, looked to save himself first. Zahn, who became a businessman in peacetime, lost only his German shepherd Hassan. Measured against the roughly five thousand children who drowned, froze to death, or were trampled in the corridors, the births reported after the disaster, including mine, hardly register; I don't count.

Most of the survivors were unloaded in Sassnitz, on the island of Rügen, in Kolberg and Swinemünde. Not a few died on board. Some of the living and the dead had to return to Gotenhafen, where the living had to wait to be transported by other refugee ships. From the end of February on, Danzig was the site of fierce fighting; the city burned, releasing floods of refugees, who up to the end crowded the piers where steamers, barges, and fishing cutters were tied up.

Early in the morning of 31 January the torpedo boat *Löwe* docked in the harbor of Kolberg. Along with Mother and her babe in arms named Paul, Heinz Köhler disembarked. He was one of the four battling captains of the lost ship and put an end to his life when the war was barely over.

The weak, the sick, and all those with frostbitten feet were taken away in ambulances. It was typical of Mother that she counted herself among those who could walk. Every time her neverending story came to the episode in which she went ashore, she would say, "All I had on my feet was stockings, but then a grandma who was a refugee too dug a pair of shoes out of a suitcase. She was sitting on top of a handcart at the side of the road and hadn't a clue where we'd come from or what all we'd been through..."

That may be true. In the Reich the sinking of the once beloved KDF ship was not reported. Such news might have weakened the will to stay the course. There were only rumors. The Soviet supreme command likewise found reasons not to publish in the Red Banner Fleet's daily bulletin the success achieved by U-boat *S-13* and its commander.

Apparently Aleksandr Marinesko was disappointed when he returned to Turku Harbor and found that he was not welcomed as befitted a hero, even though he had resumed his mission and had sunk another ship, the former ocean liner *General von Steuben,* with two torpedoes fired from the stern on 10 February. The fifteen-thousand-ton ship, traveling from Pillau with over a thousand refugees and two thousand wounded—those numbers, again—sank, bow first, in seven minutes. About three hundred survivors were counted. Some of the critically wounded were lying cheek by jowl on the upper deck of the rapidly sinking ship. They slid overboard in their cots. Marinesko had staged this attack from fighting depth, using the periscope.

Still the high command of the Baltic Red Banner Fleet hesitated to name the doubly successful captain a "hero of the Soviet Union" when his boat returned to its base. The hesitation continued. While the captain and his crew waited in vain for the traditional banquet—roast suckling pig, copious amounts of vodka—the war continued on all fronts, nearing Kolberg on the Pomeranian front. For the time being, Mother and I were billeted in a school, of which she later remarked, "At least it was warm and cozy there. Your cradle was an old desk with a hinged top. I thought to myself, my Paulie's starting his schooling mighty early..."

After the school was hit by artillery and became uninhabitable, we found shelter in a casemate. Kolberg had a reputation rooted in history as a city and fortress. In Napoleon's time, its walls and bastions had enabled it to resist his armies, for which reason the Propaganda Ministry had chosen it as the setting for a stay-the-course film, *Kolberg,* with Heinrich George playing the lead and other top Ufa stars. Throughout what remained of the Reich, this film, in color, was shown in all the cinemas that had not yet been bombed: heroic struggle against overwhelming odds.

Now, at the end of February, Kolberg's history was being repeated. Soon the city, harbor, and beach area were encircled by units of the Red Army and a Polish division. Under artillery bombardment, the effort got under way to evacuate by sea the civilian population and the refugees with whom the city was packed. Again huge crowds swarming over all the docks. But Mother refused to get on a ship ever again. "They could've beaten me with truncheons and they still wouldn't have got me on one of them boats...," she would tell anyone who asked how she escaped with a baby from the besieged and burning city. "Well, there's always a hole you can slip through," she would reply. And in fact Mother never did set foot on a boat again, even during company outings on Lake Schwerin.

In mid-March she must have sneaked past the Russian positions, carrying only a rucksack and me; or perhaps the Russian patrols took pity on the young woman and her nursling and simply let us through. If I describe myself here, in a moment of renewed flight, as a nursling, that is only partially accurate: Mother's breasts had nothing to offer me. On the torpedo boat, an East Prussian woman who recently gave birth helped out: she had more than enough milk. After that it was a woman who had lost her baby along the way. And later, too—for the duration of our flight and beyond—I lay time and again at other women's breasts.

By now all the cities along the Pomeranian coast were either occupied by the enemy or under siege; Stettin was encircled, but Swinemünde was still holding out. Farther to the east, Danzig, Zoppot, Gotenhafen had fallen. Toward the coast, units of the 2nd Soviet Army had cordoned off the Hela Peninsula near Putzig, and farther to the west, at the Oder River, Küstrin was already the scene of fierce fighting. The Greater German Reich was shrinking on all sides. At the confluence of the Rhine and the Mosel, Koblenz was in American hands. But the bridge at Remagen had finally collapsed.

Along the eastern front, Heeresgruppe Mitte reported further withdrawals in Silesia and the increasingly critical situation of the fortress city of Breslau. To make things worse, the attacks by squadrons of American and British bombers on the large and medium-sized cities continued unabated. While to the delight of Britain's Marshal Harris of the RAF, the ruins of the city of Dresden were still smoking, bombs fell on Berlin, Regensburg, Bochum, Wuppertal... Repeated targets were reservoir dams. And refugees streamed in all directions, but with a general thrust from east to west. They did not know where it was safe to stop.

Mother, too, had no particular destination in mind when she managed to get out of Kolberg with me, her most important piece of baggage, constantly whimpering because of the lack of mother's milk. Mother got caught between the front lines, managed to make some headway at night, hitching rides for short stretches in freight cars or in the Wehrmacht's bucket cars, but also often on foot among others toiling along with less and less baggage. She kept going, frequently having to throw herself to the ground as dive-bombers swooped down, trying to get as far as possible from the coast, and— always on the lookout for mothers with surplus milk— made her way to Schwerin. She described her escape route to me sometimes one way, sometimes another. Actually she intended to continue on, crossing the Elbe into the West, but we got hung up in the undestroyed capital of the Reichgau of Mecklenburg. That was at the end of April, when the Führer did away with himself.

Later, as a journeyman carpenter and surrounded by men, Mother would say, when asked about her escape route, "I could write a novel. The worst was the bombers, when they came in real low over us and pow-pow-pow...But I was always lucky. I'm telling you, it would take a lot more than that to do me in!"

That would bring her back to her main topic, the everlastingly sinking ship. Nothing else mattered. Even the cramped conditions in our next temporary housing—another school—weren't worth complaining about, since by now she knew that she and her Paulie had found refuge in the birthplace of the man after whom the ill-fated ship had been named in times of apparent peace. His name was everywhere. Even the secondary school to which we had been assigned was named after him. When we came to Schwerin, his presence could not be missed. On the southern bank of the lake, that grove of honor with the glacial boulders was still standing, and in it the large block of granite placed there in '37 to honor the martyr. I am sure that was why Mother stayed in Schwerin with me.

It's still striking that in those realms of the Internet where I usually roamed nothing stirred for a while once the ship's sinking had been celebrated retroactively, yet as if it were a current event, and all the dead had been counted up, accounted for, made to count, depending on the accounting principles used, then compared with the number of survivors, and finally contrasted with the much smaller number of those who died on the *Titanic*. I was starting to think the server had crashed, had run out of juice, that my son had had enough, that Mother's prompting had nothing to add now that the ship had gone down. But the silence was deceptive. Suddenly he was back, presenting the familiar material on a re-designed home page.

This time pictures dominated the site. In fairly grainy reproduction but captioned in bold letters, the towering block of granite presented itself for the whole world to admire, with the name of the martyr chiseled into the rock beneath the jagged S-shaped rune for victory. The martyr's importance was illustrated by means of a chronology, a list of his organizational accomplishments, testimonials embellished with exclamation points, all incorporated into the ongoing project, leading up to the day and hour of his murder in the famous health resort for tuberculosis sufferers, Davos.

As if on command or under some other compulsion, David spoke up. Initially his topic was not the monument but the martyr's murderer. David announced triumphantly that in March 1945 things took a positive turn for David Frankfurter, incarcerated for over nine years by then. After a futile attempt to have his case reopened, the Berne attorneys Brunschwig and Raas submitted a petition for clemency, addressed to the Graubünden parliament. My son's adversary had to concede that the request for reducing the eighteen-year sentence to time served was not granted until 1 June 1945, in other words, after the war was over. He explained that the decision had to wait until Switzerland's grandiose neighbor was brought to its knees. Because David Frankfurter was expelled from Switzerland after his release, he decided to go straight from the looms of Sennhof Prison to Palestine, hoping for a future Israel.

On this topic the sniping between the two grim online opponents remained fairly moderate. Konny conceded generously, "Israel is okay. It was the perfect place for that murdering Jew. He could make himself useful, on a kibbutz or something." All in all, he had nothing against Israel. He even admired the toughness of its army. And he completely supported the Israelis' determination to take a hard line. They had no other choice. When dealing with Palestinians and such Muslims, you couldn't give an inch. Sure, if all the Jews would just pack up and move to the Promised Land, like that murdering Jew Frankfurter, he would be all for it: "Then the rest of the world would be Jew-free!"

David accepted this horrendous notion; he agreed with my son in theory. Apparently he was worried: as far as the safety of the Jewish citizens of Germany was concerned—and he included himself among them—he feared the worst; anti-Semitism was increasing by leaps and bounds. Once again one had to think about leaving the country. "I, too, will be packing my bags soon..." Whereupon Konny wished him "Bon voyage" but then hinted that it would give him pleasure if the occasion arose for him to meet his bosom enemy before the latter's departure—not just online: "We should get together, check each other out, preferably sooner rather than later..."

He even proposed a meeting place, but left the date for the desired rendezvous open. At the spot where the block of granite had towered above the others in the memorial grove, and where today hardly anything preserved the memory of the martyr, because desecrators had cleared away the rock and the hall of honor—in that very place where, in the not-too-distant future, a stone monument would have to be erected once more, in that historically meaningful place they should meet.

The sniping promptly resumed. David favored a meeting anywhere but in that accursed location. "I absolutely reject your historical revisionism..." My son added his own fuel to the fire: "He who forgets his people's past is not worthy of it!" David agreed with that. What followed was sheer silliness. They even allowed themselves to make jokes. To one of them—"What's the difference between e-mail and Emil?"—I unfortunately did not get the punch line. I logged out too soon.

I've been there numerous times. Most recently a few weeks back, as if I were the perpetrator, as if I had to keep returning to the scene of the crime, as if the father were running after the son.

From Mölln, where neither Gabi nor I could find much to say to each other, to Ratzeburg. From there I drove east, passing through Mustin, a tiny village just beyond which the border had been located, complete with death strip, cutting off the highway. One still sees a three-hundred-meter gap in the chestnuts planted long ago on either side of the road: not a tree to right or left. The place gives one a feel for the multitiered efforts the Workers' and Peasants' State undertook to secure its people.

Once I left that scar in the landscape behind me, Mecklenburg's sweeping farmland extended all the way to the horizon on both sides of the once more tree-lined highway. Hardly any undulations, few larger stands of trees. On the outskirts of Gadebusch I took the new bypass. A strip of home improvement stores, shopping centers, flat-roofed auto dealerships, trying with strings of drooping pennants to revive business. The Wild East! Not until close to Schwerin, where the road was now lined with smaller varieties of trees, did the area become hilly. I drove past larger wooded stretches, the radio tuned to channel 3: the classical request program.

I then turned right onto Route 106, toward Ludwigslust, and was soon approaching the Grosser Dreesch housing complex, thrown up in several stages and once home to fifty thousand citizens of the GDR, and parked my Mazda by unit 3, right next to the Lenin monument in the curve at the end of Gagarinstrasse. The weather held; it didn't rain. Now renovated and made presentable with pastel colors, the apartment buildings lined up in a row.

Every time I visit Mother, I am amazed that this bronze statue, which grew so large under the hands of its Estonian creator, is still standing. Although Lenin is gazing westward, he was denied any gesture that might indicate a destination. With both hands in his coat pockets, he stands there like a man out for a stroll who is allowing himself to take a breather, his feet resting on the low granite platform that forms a pedestal. The left corner of its lowest step is clad in bronze. The inscription molded into the metal in capital letters recalls a revolutionary resolution: THE LAND REFORM DECREE. Only on the front does Lenin's overcoat reveal traces of color from some meaningless spray-can graffiti. Pigeon droppings on the shoulders. His wrinkled trousers have remained clean.

I did not linger on Gagarinstrasse. Mother lives on the eleventh floor, with a balcony and a view of the nearby broadcast tower. She insisted on serving me coffee, which she always makes too strong. After the renovation of the concrete-slab buildings, the rents were raised—to manageable levels, Mother thinks. We talked about that, only that. Otherwise there was not much to say. She did not ask what had brought me to the city of many lakes, besides my brief visit to her: "Certainly not the Führer's birthday!" The date of my arrival must have given my destination away; she exclaimed as I entered her apartment—and after I had denied myself a glance into Konny's room: "What's there for you? Nothing to be done about it now."

Taking Hamburger Allee, formerly Lenin-Allee, I drove in the direction of the zoo, then along Am Hexenberg, and parked by the youth hostel, having found my way to the spot as if in a trance. Around the back of the gray stuccoed structure from the early fifties, the wooded bank on the southern end of Lake Schwerin falls off steeply. Down below, almost at the water's edge, you see Franzosenweg, a favorite path for walkers and bicycle riders.

A sunny day by now. Actually not typical April weather. When the sun came out, it had real warmth. At a slight distance from the entrance to the youth hostel, the moss-covered blocks of granite still lay motionless, as though nothing had happened, remnants of the memorial grove that had been cleared away, not very thoroughly, decades earlier. Among the trees once planted to form the grove, scanty underbrush. The square foundation of the hall of honor was easy to make out, because only a little dirt had been dumped over it, but the youth hostel faced the site, obstructing any sense of the original layout. To the left of the hostel's entrance, above which one could read in raised lettering the name of the hostel, "Kurt Bürger," a Ping-Pong table on sawhorses was waiting for players. A sign on the door hung slightly crooked: CLOSED FROM 9 AM TO 4 PM.

I stood for a long time amid the mossy blocks of granite, one of which even displayed fragments of an inscription and a chiseled rune. Lost property—from what century?

Back in the day when Mother and I found refuge in Schwerin, everything was still standing: boulder next to boulder, the Nazi hall of honor, and the massive piece of granite with the martyr's name. When Mother first saw the memorial, it was already neglected, but still under the care of the Party, which was crumbling from the outside in. She told me that she came upon the oaks and beeches, still small at the time, while she was out looking for firewood: "Where they assigned us to, there wasn't a blessed thing to burn in the stove…" Many other women and children were also out looking. By the time the American tanks reached Schwerin from their bridgehead on the Elbe southwest of Boizenburg, followed by the British—"They had genuine Scotch soldiers…"—we had been moved from the cellar of the school to Lehmstrasse, in the part of town known as the Schelfstadt; it must have been fairly run-down by the end of the war. We were assigned to a brick outbuilding with a tar-paper roof, located, of course, to the rear of the building that fronted on the street. It's still standing, that shack. We had two tiny rooms and a kitchen. You had to go out to the courtyard to use the toilet. They even put in a cylinder stove for us. The stovepipe went through the kitchen window. And to feed the stove—Mother cooked on the cover plate—she had to hunt all over for firewood.

That's how she happened upon the memorial grove. When the British pulled out in June and the Red Army came in, and stayed for good, the boulders with various names and runes chiseled on them remained standing for a long time; the Russians didn't care.

Since the Potsdam conference, where the victors divided up Germany, we were in the Soviet occupation zone, Mother even of her own free will, ever since she discovered, on the largest of the remaining stones, set close to the lakeshore, a name that was not unfamiliar: "That stone had the same name as our *Yustloff* ..."

On my last visit to Schwerin, when I stood amid the mossy granite blocks in front of a split boulder and could puzzle out what was left of the name Wilhelm Dahl in cuneiform script—of the first name, only the syllable "helm" was left, next to the split edge—I succumbed to the temptation to picture Mother out hunting for firewood, and coming, with her arms full of branches and twigs, upon the still intact grove and the open memorial hall. On the dozen or so glacial boulders lined up there, she would have deciphered the names of Party members unfamiliar to her but obviously deserving, among them the Kreisleiter of Wismar, Wilhelm Dahl. I see her, small in stature and emaciated, too, standing astonished before the four-meter-high rock, but I can't guess her thoughts, which may have become tangled once she read the inscription on the martyr's stone. But if I know Mother, she certainly didn't hesitate for a moment to step inside the memorial hall in the middle of the grove.

Formed of square granite blocks, it had been built directly on the ground. Into the smooth outside surfaces of the square columns that supported the hall on its open sides, a contemporary sculptor had chiseled SA standard-bearers in outline, larger than life. Affixed to the walls on the interior of the roofless structure were also ten bronze plaques with the names of the dead who were honored there. Eight of the names carried the notation "murdered" after the date of death. The floor of the hall was filthy. Mother told me, "It was full of dog shit..."

The granite block for Wilhelm Gustloff, however, stood apart from the row of boulders, at a spot that could be seen from the open memorial hall as particularly significant. From there one had a wide-angle view of the lake. Mother no doubt looked in a different direction. And I was never there when she was out hunting for wood. During her search for anything burnable, a woman from the neighborhood was probably nursing me; her name was Frau Kurbjun. Mother, after all, hardly had a bosom, then or later, just two pointy little pouches.

That's how it goes with monuments. Some of them are put up too soon, and then, when the era of their particular notion of heroism is past, have to be cleared away. Others, like the Lenin statue by the Grosser Dreesch complex, at the corner of Hamburger Allee and Plater Strasse, remain standing. And the monument to the commander of submarine *S-13* went up in St. Petersburg barely a decade ago, on 8 May 1990, forty-five years after the end of the war and twenty-seven years after Marinesko's death: a triangular granite column supports the larger-than-life bareheaded bronze bust of the man belatedly designated a "hero of the Soviet Union."

Former naval officers, by then retired, had established committees in Odessa, Moscow, and elsewhere and persistently petitioned for recognition of the captain, who had died in '63. In Königsberg, as Kaliningrad was called until the end of the war, the bank of the Pregel River behind the Regional Museum was even named after him. That street still bears his name, while the Schlossgartenallee in Schwerin, which from '37 on was called Wilhelm-Gustloff-Allee, still leads to the vicinity of the former memorial grove, but under its old name; similarly, since the fall of the Wall, Lenin-Allee has become Hamburger Allee, and runs through the Grosser Dreesch concrete-slab complex, past the steadfast statue of Lenin. On the other hand, Mother's address, which celebrates the cosmonaut Yuri Gagarin, has remained true to itself.

There is a notable omission. Nothing has been named after the medical student David Frankfurter. No street, no school bears his name. Nowhere was a monument erected to the murderer of Wilhelm Gustloff. No Web site campaigned for a David-and-Goliath sculpture, perhaps in Davos, the scene of the crime. And if my son's bosom enemy had posted such a demand on the Net, the hate pages would certainly have called for the monument to be cleared away by a shaven-headed special operations commando.

That's how it's always been. Nothing lasts forever. Yet the district administration of the NSDAP in Schwerin and the city's mayor went to great trouble after Gustloff's murder to design a memorial grove that would be there for eternity. As early as December 1936, when the trial of Frankfurter was wrapped up in Chur and the verdict reached, the search was under way in the fields of Mecklenburg for glacial boulders to form an enclosure around the memorial grove. The instructions read, "For this purpose natural stones in every size are required, of the sort found near buildings and on native soil around Schwerin..." And a letter written by the Gau's coordinator of ideological training reveals that the regional capital felt obligated to support the Gau administration financially, to the tune of "a subsidy of 10,000 reichsmarks."

On 10 September 1949, when the dismantling of the grove of honor and the relocation of the corpses and urns was as good as complete, the mayor wrote on his de-Nazified letterhead to the regional government, revealing that this operation had been less costly: "Expenditures of 6,096.75 marks are hereby reported to the regional government for purposes of reimbursement..."

One also discovers that the "residual ashes of Wilhelm Gustloff" could not be transferred to the municipal burial ground: "According to the statement of master mason Kröpelin, G.'s urn is located in the foundation of the stone memorial. Removal of the urn is not possible at this time..."

The removal did not take place until the early fifties, shortly before the youth hostel was built and named in memory of the antifascist Kurt Bürger, recently deceased. Around this time, the U-boat hero Marinesko had already spent three years in Siberia. Right after *S-13* sailed into the Finnish harbor of Turku, and the crew went ashore, trouble began for the man who wanted to be celebrated as a hero. Although the NKVD file and the misconduct that had not yet been dealt with in court continued to hang over him, he did not cease, whether cold sober or disinhibited by vodka, to demand recognition for his deeds. Although *S-13* was designated a Distinguished Red Banner Boat, and all the crew members received the Order of the War for the Fatherland to pin on their chests, as well another medal, that of the Red Flag, whose motif was the star, hammer, and sickle, Aleksandr Marinesko was not declared a Hero of the Soviet Union. Worse yet, the official bulletins of the Baltic Red Banner Fleet continued to make absolutely no mention of the sinking of the twenty-five-thousand-ton *Wilhelm Gustloff,* and not a word testified to the rapid sinking of the *General von Steuben.*

It was as if the tubes in the bow and stern of the submarine had fired phantom torpedoes at nonexistent targets. The twelve thousand or more dead registered to his account didn't count. Was the naval high command embarrassed because of the only roughly calculable number of drowned children, women, and severely wounded soldiers? Or had Marinesko's successes got lost in the intoxication of victory that characterized the last months of the war, with their surfeit of heroic deeds? But now his loud insistence could not be ignored. Nothing could deter him from playing up his successes whenever the occasion presented itself. He became a nuisance.

In September 1945 he was relieved of the command of his submarine, and soon thereafter he was degraded to the rank of lieutenant. In October he was discharged from the Soviet navy. The justification given for this three-stage dishonorable discharge was "an indifferent and negligent attitude toward his duties."

When his application to the merchant marine was rejected—on the pretext that he was nearsighted in one eye—Marinesko found employment as the administrator of a supply depot responsible for the distribution of building materials. Before long he saw fit to accuse the director of the collective—with insufficient evidence— of having taken bribes, paid kickbacks to Party functionaries, and trafficked in materials, whereupon Marinesko came under suspicion of violating the law himself by being too generous in giving away only slightly damaged building materials. A special court sentenced him to three years at hard labor. He was deported to Kolyma on the East Siberian Sea, a place that belonged to the Gulag Archipelago, whose daily routine has been written about. Not until two years after Stalin's death did he put Siberia behind him, in a topographical sense. He came back ill. But it wasn't until the early sixties that the damaged U-boat hero was rehabilitated. He was restored to the rank of captain third class, retired and entitled to a pension.

Now I must repeat myself by reverting to something already mentioned. That is why I write here: when Stalin's death was reported in the East and West, I saw Mother cry. She even lit candles. Eight years old at the time, I was standing at the kitchen table and didn't have to be in school, having just got over the measles or something else that itched, was peeling potatoes, which were supposed to go on the table with margarine and curd cheese, and saw Mother crying behind burning candles over Stalin's death. Potatoes, candles, and tears were scarce in those days. Throughout my childhood on Lehmstrasse, and as long as I was in secondary school in Schwerin, I never saw her cry again. When Mother had cried her eyes out, her face took on an absent expression, her I'm-not-home look, which Aunt Jenny remembered from their early years. At the carpentry shop on Langfuhr's Elsenstrasse they would comment, "Tulla's gone and bashed in the windows again."

After she had cried long enough for the death of the great comrade Stalin, and then had no expression for a while, we ate the boiled potatoes she had fixed, with curd cheese and a pat of margarine.

Around this time Mother took her master's test and soon became the leader of a carpentry brigade in the Schwerin furniture plant, which produced bedroom furniture according to quota, with instructions to deliver it to the Soviet Union in the spirit of friendship between our peoples. Blurry though her image may have been at the time, to tell the truth, Mother has remained a Stalinist to this day, though when I bring this up in an argument, she tries to downplay her hero to appease his critics: "He was just a human being, you know..."

And around this time, while Marinesko remained at the mercy of the Siberian climate and conditions in the Soviet penal camps, while Mother kept faith with Stalin, and I took pride in my Young Pioneers' neckerchief,

David Frankfurter, cured in the penitentiary of his supposedly chronic osteomyelitis, was making himself useful as an official in Israel's defense ministry. In the meantime he had married. Later two children came along.

And something else happened during these years: Hedwig Gustloff, the widow of the murdered Wilhelm, left Schwerin. From then on she lived west of the border separating the two Germanys, in Lübeck. The glazed-brick house at 14 Sebastian-Bach-Strasse, which the couple built shortly before the murder, had been expropriated soon after the war. I saw a picture of the building, a typical solid single-family house, on the Internet. My son went so far as to post on his Web site the demand that the illegally expropriated house be turned into a "Gustloff Museum" and opened to the interested public. Far beyond Schwerin the need existed for expertly displayed factual information. For all he cared, a bronze plaque could be mounted to the left of the window of the enclosed balcony, announcing that from 1945 to 1951 the first prime minister of Mecklenburg, a certain Wilhelm Höcker, had lived in the expropriated house. He would have no objection to including wording such as "after the crushing of Hitler-fascism." That was a fact, after all, as the martyr's murder remained a fact.

My son was clever at positioning pictures and icons, tables and documents. Thus one could view on his Web site not only the front but also the back of the mighty granite boulder erected on the southern shore of Lake Schwerin. He had gone to the trouble of providing an enlargement of the chiseled inscription that was barely legible on the photograph showing the entire stone from the rear. Three lines, one above the other: LIVED FOR THE MOVEMENT — MURDERED BY A JEW — DIED FOR GERMANY. Since the middle line not only suppressed the name of the perpetrator but explicitly characterized Jews generically as murderers, it could be assumed that in zeroing in on this detail—the interpretation offered later— Konny revealed that he had overcome his fixation on the historical David Frankfurter and wanted to demonstrate his hatred for "Jewry in toto."

Yet this explanation, as well as further searches for a motive, hardly shed any light on what occurred on the afternoon of 20 April 1997. In front of the youth hostel, closed at this time of year and seemingly lifeless, something happened that was not predestined yet played itself out on the mossy foundation of the former memorial hall as if rehearsed.

Whatever had induced the virtual David to respond to a vague invitation and travel, in the flesh, by train all the way from Karlsruhe, where the eighteen-year-old schoolboy lived with his parents, the eldest of three sons? And what had got into Konny to make him seek an actual encounter that would convert into a reality a bosom-enemy relationship that had developed over the Internet and was essentially a fiction? The invitation to the meeting had been slipped so surreptitiously into the rubbish that constituted their communication that it could have been picked up only by the intimate adversary who signed himself David.

Once the youth hostel was rejected as a meeting place, the two of them accepted a compromise. They would meet where the martyr had been born. A good question for a quiz, because my son's Web site named neither a city, nor a street, nor a house number. Nonetheless, the reference presented no problem to someone familiar with the material; and David, like Konny, who called himself Wilhelm online, knew even the most banal details of the damned Gustloff story. As would become apparent during the visit, he even knew that the secondary school Wilhelm Gustloff had attended and that had been named for him after his death was called Peace School since GDR times. My son not only respected his adversary's comprehensive expertise; he also admired him for being a "perfectionist."

And so they met, on a beautiful spring day, on Martinstrasse, in front of number 2, at the corner of Wismarsche Strasse. David had accepted without comment the particular date Wilhelm chose. Their meeting took place in front of a recently restored stucco facade, intended to make one forget the years and years of decay. They are said to have greeted each other with a handshake, after which David introduced himself to the tall, lanky Konrad Pokriefke as David Stremplin.

The next item on the agenda was a stroll through the town, on Konny's suggestion. During their visit to the Schelfstadt, whose name recalls the reeds that once grew thickly along the banks of the lake on which it borders, the visitor was even shown, as if it were a special attraction, the brick shack with a tar-paper roof, located in a rear courtyard on Lehmstrasse, where Mother and I lived after the war; he was also shown the still crumbling and the already renovated half-timber houses in that picturesque quarter. Konny led David to all the sites and secret hiding places of my youth, as unerringly as though they had been his own.

After St. Nicholas's, the Schelfstadt church, which they viewed from the inside and outside, they of course had to take in the castle on Castle Island. There was no rush. My son made no attempt to hurry things along. He even suggested that they visit the museum next to the castle, but his guest showed no interest, grew impatient, was now intent on seeing the site in front of the youth hostel.

Nonetheless they took a break during their stroll through the town. At a Italian ice cream cafe each of them downed a good-sized portion of gelato. As the host, Konny picked up the tab. And David Stremplin is said to have talked amiably, but with ironic detachment, about his parents, a nuclear physicist and a music teacher. I am willing to bet that my son said not a word about his father and mother; but no doubt the tale of his grandmother's miraculous survival was important enough to be brought up.

Then the two bosom enemies, unequal in height—David tended more toward the horizontal, and was a head shorter—made their way through the castle park, passed the grinding mill, walked along Schlossgarten-allee, which had become an exclusive address, with villas spruced up in gleaming white, and then by way of

Waldschulweg approached the scene of the crime, a fairly level area under trees. Initially there was no tension. David Stremplin is said to have praised the view of the lake. If a ball and rackets had been lying on the Ping-Pong table in front of the youth hostel, they might have played; Konny and David were both passionate about table tennis and would hardly have missed such an opportunity. Perhaps a quick volley over the net would have proved relaxing, and the afternoon might have taken a different course.

Then they were standing on historic ground, so to speak. Yet even the moss-covered blocks of granite and the fragment of the boulder with the chiseled rune and traces of a name did not provide sufficient pretext for a quarrel. The two even laughed in two-part harmony at a squirrel leaping from beech tree to beech tree. Not until they were standing on the foundation of the old hall of honor, and my son explained to his guest exactly where the large memorial stone had stood—behind the youth hostel, which had not been there in those days— only then, when he indicated the sight line for the granite boulder, and recited the martyr's name on the front of the stone and then, word for word, the three lines inscribed on the back, did David Stremplin allegedly say, "As a Jew, I have only this to say," whereupon he spat three times on the mossy foundation—thereby, as my son later testified, "desecrating" the memorial site.

Right after that, shots were fired. In spite of the sunny day, Konny was wearing a parka. From one of its roomy pockets, the one on the right, he pulled the weapon and fired four times. It was a Russian-made pistol. The first shot struck the stomach, the following ones the head. David Stremplin tumbled backward without a word. Later my son made a point of saying that he had struck his victim as many times as the Jew Frankfurter, long ago in Davos. And like him, he went to the nearest telephone booth, dialed the emergency number, and reported his crime. Without returning to the scene, he set out for the police station, where he turned himself in with the words, "I fired because I am a German."

On his way there, he saw a patrol car and an ambulance approaching, blue lights flashing. But help arrived too late for David Stremplin.

8

HE, WHO CLAIMS TO KNOW ME, CONTENDS THAT I don't know my own flesh and blood. Maybe it is true that I had no access to his innermost torture chambers. That I was not smart enough to decipher my son's secrets. Not until the trial began did I get closer to Konny— if not an arm's length away, at least within shouting distance—but I couldn't bring myself to call out to him on the witness stand helpful things like, "Your father stands by you!" or, "Don't lecture them, son. Cut it short!"

That's probably why a certain someone insists on calling me a "Johnny-come-lately father." Everything that I try to crabwalk away from, or admit to in relative proximity to the truth, or reveal as if under duress, comes out, as he sees it, "after the fact and from a guilty conscience."

And now that all my efforts have been stamped TOO LATE, he is combing through my messy piles of documents, this hodgepodge of note cards, and wants to know what became of Mother's fox stole. This postscript I still owe him seems particularly important to him, the boss; he tells me not to withhold any of the details I know, but to tell the story of Tulla's fox blow by blow, no matter how I hate that now unfashionable piece of clothing.

It's true. Mother owned one from the beginning, and still wears it. She was about sixteen, a streetcar conductor with a two-pointed cap and a block of tickets, doing her shift on lines 5 and 2, when, at the Hochstriess stop, she received a gift from a corporal who is another of my possible fathers: the complete fox pelt, already prepared by the furrier. "He came back wounded from the Arctic front, and now he was in Oliva on leave to recuperate," was and is her shorthand depiction of the man who may have fathered me, for neither the sinister Harry Liebenau nor some immature Luftwaffe auxiliary could have come up with the idea of giving Mother a fox stole.

It was with this warm stole around her neck that she boarded the *Gustloff* when the Pokriefkes were allowed to get on. Shortly after the ship cast off, when the pregnant girl, leaning on a dreadfully young naval recruit, ventured onto the ice-coated sundeck, taking one step at a time, she was wearing the fur. The fox was close at hand, next to the life jacket, as she lay in the maternity ward and Dr. Richter gave her an injection, right after the third torpedo struck and the contractions began. And with nothing else—the rucksack was left behind—but the life jacket buckled on and the fox around her neck, Mother—who wasn't Mother yet—scrambled into the lifeboat and claims she had reached for the fox before the life jacket.

That was how she came on board the torpedo boat

Löwe, shoeless but warmed by the fur. And only during the birth, which began soon afterward, that is, at the very minute when the *Gustloff* sank, first the bow and then capsizing to the port side, whereupon the cry of the countless thousands blended with my first cry, only then did the fur again lie next to her, rolled up. But when she left the torpedo boat in Kolberg, her hair having turned white at one blow, Mother might have been wearing only stockings as she carried her baby, but she had the fox, which no shock had bleached, wound around her neck like a choker.

She claims that during the long flight from the Russians she wrapped me in the fur to protect me against the bitter cold. Without the fox I would certainly have frozen to death in the horde of refugees backed up at the bridge over the Oder. I owe my life to the fox alone—not to the women with surplus milk. "Without that there you'd've been a lump of ice..." And the corporal who had conferred the fur on her—allegedly the work of a furrier in Warsaw—is said to have remarked in parting, "Who knows what it'll be good for someday, girl."

In peacetime, however, when we no longer had to freeze, the fox-red fur belonged only to her, lay in the wardrobe in a shoe box. She wore it on suitable and unsuitable occasions. For instance, when she received her master's diploma, then when she earned recognition as a "deserving activist," even at company celebrations, when "evening entertainment" was on the schedule. And when I had had my fill of the Workers' and Peasants' State and wanted to go to the West by way of East Berlin, she came with me to the station with the fox around her neck. Later, much later, when, after a small eternity, the border was gone and Mother was receiving her pension, she appeared at the survivors' reunion in the Baltic coastal resort of Damp with her always-well-cared-for fox; she certainly looked unusual among the other women her age, who were rigged out in the latest styles.

And on the first day of the trial, when all that happened was that the charges were read and my son admitted everything without reservation, but saw himself as beyond guilt—"I did what I had to do!"—and Mother did not join Gabi and me, who had to sit together, willy-nilly, but made a show of going to sit with the parents of David, mortally wounded by four shots, she was of course wearing the fox nestled around her neck like a noose. Its pointed little snout had its teeth buried in the skin above the root of the tail, and the deceptively real glass eyes, one of which had been lost during the flight and had to be replaced, lay at an oblique angle to Mother's light gray eyes, with the result that a double gaze fastened on the accused or the judge's bench.

It always embarrassed me to see her in this old-fashioned getup, the more so because the fox did not smell of Mother's favorite perfume, Tosca, but insistently and at all seasons of mothballs; and by now the creature looked fairly scruffy, too. But when she was called on the second day as a witness for the defense and stepped up to the witness stand, even I was impressed: like an anorexic diva, she wore the colorful fur to contrast with her blazing white hair, and introduced her first answers with the formula "I swear...," even though she had not been put under oath, after which she said everything she had to say with seeming effortlessness, if a bit stiltedly, in High German.

In contrast to Gabi and me, who took advantage of our right as parents to refuse to provide any information, Mother had plenty to say. Before the entire court—that is, before three judges—the presiding judge and the associate judges—as well as the two juvenile court magistrates, she spoke as if she were at a religious revival. People listened to her as she crucified the state's attorney for juvenile cases. Basically, this terrible deed had hit her hard, too. Since it occurred, her heart had been torn asunder. A fiery sword had sliced through her. She had been crushed by a mighty fist.

On Demmlerplatz, where the trial was taking place in the regional courthouse's large juvenile courtroom, Mother presented herself as emotionally and spiritually devastated. After cursing fate, she generously dispensed praise and blame. She blamed the parents for being incapable of loving their child, and praised her grandson, misled by forces of evil and that devilish invention, "that computer thingamabob," as hardworking and polite, cleaner than clean, always helpful and remarkably punctual, and not only when it was a question of coming to supper. She swore that since her grandson Konrad had been around—and she had had this joy since his fifteenth year—even she had taken to organizing her day down to the minute. Yes, she had to admit it: she had been the one who gave him the computer thingamabob, with all the bells and whistles. Not that the boy had been spoiled by his grandmother, on the contrary. It was because he had turned out to be so exceptionally undemanding that she had been glad to fulfill his desire for this "modern contraption." "He never asked for anything else!" she exclaimed, and recalled, "My Konradchen could keep himself entertained for hours with that thing."

Then, after she had cursed all that seductive modern stuff, she came to her real topic. The ship, that is, which not a soul had wanted to hear about, had inspired her grandson to ask countless questions. But "Konradchen" had not merely shown an interest in the sinking "of the beautiful KDF steamer full of women and little children," and it was not about that alone that he had interrogated his grandmother, the survivor; rather he had been eager, and not least in response to her expressed desire, to spread his vast knowledge, "the whole kit and caboodle," by means of the computer she had given him, all the way to Australia and Alaska. "That is not prohibited, Your Honor, is it?" Mother exclaimed, and jerked the fox's head to the middle of her chest.

Then she got around to speaking of the victim, almost in passing. It had pleased her that her "Konradchen" had made friends this way—"through that computer thingamabob, I mean"—with another boy, without knowing him personally, even if the two often disagreed, because otherwise her beloved grandchild was generally considered a loner. And that's what he was. Even his re-

lationship with his little girlfriend from Ratzeburg—
"she helps out at a dentist's"—had to be seen as not too
serious—"There hasn't been any sex and such," of that
she was sure.

All that and more Mother said in fairly correct High
German as a witness for the defense, making an obvious
effort to sound refined. Konrad's "sensitive approach to
questions of conscience," his "unbending love of the
truth," and his "unswerving pride in Germany" were
lauded to the court. But when Mother affirmed how
little it mattered to her that Konrad's computer friend
had been a Jewish boy, the state's attorney for juvenile
cases assured her that it had been known for quite a
while, and documented as well, that the murdered boy's
parents had no Jewish blood; rather, Father Stremplin's
father had been a pastor in Württemberg and his wife
came from a farm family that had had roots in Baden for
generations. At that Mother became visibly agitated. She
plucked at the fur, displayed for a few seconds her "I'm-
not-home" look, then abandoned all efforts to speak
High German, shouting, "What a swindle! How was
my Konradchen supposed to know that this David was
a fake Yid? So he was fooling himself and other folks,
presenting himself all the time as a real Yid and going
on and on about our guilt..."

When she castigated the murder victim as a "common liar" and "like one of them phonies from the fifties,"
the presiding judge ordered her to step down. Of course
Konny, who up to that point had been listening to
Mother's foxy affirmations with a delicate smile, seemed

by no means startled, though possibly disappointed, when the juvenile prosecutor presented for Wolfgang Stremplin—who had called himself David online—"proof of Aryan lineage," as he put it, assuming an ironic air. My son commented with calm confidence on what he already knew: "That doesn't change the situation in the least. It was up to me to decide whether the person known to me as David was speaking as a Jew and behaving as such." When the presiding judge asked him whether he had ever met a real Jew, in Mölln or in Schwerin, he replied with a clear no, but added, "That wasn't relevant to my decision. I fired as a matter of principle."

After that the questioning focused on the pistol, which after the deed my son had hurled down the steep bank into Lake Schwerin; on this subject Mother commented only briefly: "How could I have found the thing, Herr Staatsanwalt? My Konradchen always cleaned his own room. That was a point of pride with him."

Asked about the murder weapon, my son said that he had had the gun available—it was a 7-mm Tokarev, Soviet army surplus—for a year and a half. That had been necessary because radical right-wing youths from the surrounding Mecklenburg countryside had threatened him. No, he didn't want to and wouldn't name any names. "I refuse to betray former comrades!" The occasion for the threats had been a lecture that he gave on the invitation of a nationalist solidarity organization. The topic, "The Fate of the KDF Ship *Wilhelm Gustloff,* from the Laying of the Keel to the Sinking," had presumably been pitched too high for some in the audience, "among them some dumbskulls excessively fond of beer drinking." The baldies had been particularly outraged when he objectively acknowledged the military achievement of the Soviet U-boat commander, who had torpedoed the boat from a risky position. He was later harassed in public by various tough guys as a "Russian-lover," and even physically attacked. "From then on, it was clear to me that you couldn't confront these types, with their primitive Nazism, without being armed. Arguing with them got you nowhere."

The lecture, which was delivered one weekend early in '96 in a Schwerin restaurant, the meeting place for the aforementioned solidarity organization, and two further lectures he was not given permission to deliver, but which were provided to the court in hard copy, would play a role in the further course of the hearing.

As for his oral report, both of us had failed him. Gabi and I should have been aware of what had happened in Mölln, but we had both been looking the other way. Even though she taught at another school, word had to have reached Gabi that her son had been forbidden to give a report on a controversial topic because the subject matter was deemed "inappropriate." Admittedly, I too should have taken a greater interest in my son.

For instance, it would have been possible for me to schedule my visits to Mölln—which were unfortunately irregular, due to my professional obligations—so that I could have asked questions on parents' night, even if that had resulted in a confrontation with one of these narrow-minded pedants. I could have interjected, "What's this about banning a report? Don't you believe in free speech?" or something of the sort. Perhaps Konny's report, subtitled "The Positive Aspects of the Nazi Organization Strength through Joy," might have added some spice to the bland social studies curriculum. But I didn't make it to any parents' nights, and Gabi felt it would be wrong to complicate her colleagues' already difficult situation further by interfering, in her subjective role as a mother, the more so since she had declared herself "strictly opposed to any attempt to portray the Nazi pseudo-ideology as innocuous," and had always defended her leftist position to her son, often too impatiently, as she conceded.

Nothing absolves us. One can't blame everything on Mother or on the teachers' moralistic rigidity. During the proceedings, my ex and I—she rather hesitantly, and constantly invoking the limits of what can be expected of education—had to admit to our mutual failure. Oh, if only I, born fatherless, had never become a father!

It turned out that the parents of poor David—whose real name was Wolfgang and whose philo-Semitic posturing had apparently provoked our Konny—were reproaching themselves in much the same terms. At any rate, during a recess, when Gabi and I had an initially awkward but then fairly frank conversation with the couple, Herr Stremplin told me that it had probably been his purely theoretical scientific work at the nuclear research center and certainly also his overly detached attitude toward certain historical events that had resulted in the alienation between him and his son—which had reached the point that they stopped speaking to one another. In particular, his relatively dispassionate view of the period of National Socialist rule had been beyond his son's comprehension. "Well, the result was increasing distance between us."

And Frau Stremplin expressed the opinion that Wolfgang had always been an oddball. His only contact with boys his own age had come through Ping-Pong. She had never picked up any indication of relationships with girls. But relatively early, at the age of fourteen, her son adopted the name David and became so obsessed with thoughts of atonement for the wartime atrocities and mass killings, which, God knows, were constantly harped on in our society, that eventually everything Jewish became somehow sacred to him. Last year for Christmas he asked for a menorah, of all things. And it had been somehow off-putting to see him sitting in his room at his one and only love, the computer, wearing one of those little caps religious Jews wore. "He kept asking me to cook kosher!" That, at any rate, was her explanation as to why Wolfgang had represented himself in his computer games as a person of the Mosaic faith. When she objected that at some point there somehow had to be an end to these neverending accusations, she was ignored. "In the last few months our boy became unreachable." For that reason she had no idea how her son had come upon this dreadful Nazi functionary and his murderer, a medical student named Frankfurter. "Did we give up trying to have an influence on him too soon?"

Frau Stremplin spoke in bursts. Her husband nodded by way of confirmation. Wolfgang had worshipped this David Frankfurter, he said. His endless talk of David and Goliath had been silly, but apparently it was a serious matter to him. His younger brothers, Jobst and Tobias, teased him for this cult he had created. On his desk he even had a framed photo of the young man, taken shortly before the murder in Davos. And then those books, newspaper clippings, and computer printouts. Apparently it was all connected with that man Gustloff and the ship named after him. "It was somehow dreadful what happened when that ship went down. All those children. We didn't know anything about it. Not even my husband, and his hobby is research on recent German history. Even he didn't have any information on the Gustloff case, unfortunately, until..."

She cried. Gabi cried, too, and in her helplessness put her hand on Frau Stremplin's shoulder. I could have wailed, too, but the fathers made do with exchanging glances intended to signal mutual understanding. We got together with Wolfgang's parents several more times, outside the courthouse as well. Decent liberals who reproached themselves rather than us. Always making an effort to understand. It seemed to me that during the trial they listened intently to Konny's usually long-winded speeches, as if they were hoping to gain some insight from him, their son's murderer.

I found the Stremplins quite likable. He, around fifty,

with glasses and well-groomed gray hair, looked like the type who sees everything as relative, even hard and fast facts. She, in her mid-forties but looking younger than that, tended to find things somehow inexplicable. When the conversation came around to Mother, she said, "Your son's grandmother is certainly a remarkable person, but she makes an uncanny impression on me, somehow..."

We learned that Wolfgang's younger brothers were cut from a different cloth. And she was still worrying about her eldest son's performance in school, specifically his weakness in mathematics and physics, as if he were still alive, "somehow," and would soon be taking the university qualifying exams.

We sat in one of Schwerin's new upscale cafes, on bar stools at a round table that was a little too high. As if by prearrangement, we had all ordered cappuccinos. No pastry to go with them. Sometimes we drifted away from the topic, for instance when we felt we had to admit to the Stremplins, who were about our age, the reasons for our early divorce. Gabi maintained that it was normal nowadays for people to separate when things didn't work out, and there was no need to assign blame. I held back and let my ex deal with everything halfway explicable, but then I changed the subject, bringing up in a fairly confused fashion the oral reports that had been banned in Konny's schools in Mölln and Schwerin. Immediately Gabi and I were fighting again, just we had eons ago during our marriage. I argued that our son's unhappiness—and its dreadful consequences—started when he was prohibited from presenting his view of 30 January

1933, and also the social significance of the Nazi organization Strength through Joy, but Gabi interrupted me: "Perfectly understandable that the teacher had to put a stop to it. After all, in terms of that date, its real significance was that it was the day of Hitler's takeover, not that it happened to be the birthday of a minor figure, about whose importance our son wanted to go on and on, especially in conjunction with his subtopic, 'The Neglect of Monuments'..."

In court, this is what happened: the reports that were never given in Mölln and Schwerin were dealt with in the testimony of two teachers, both of whom confirmed that the defendant had been an excellent student. Unanimously—and in this respect in pan-German agreement—the two educators said that the banned reports had been severely infected with National Socialist thinking, which, to be sure, had been expressed with intelligent subtlety, for instance in the advocacy for a "classless Volk community," but also in the demand for an "ideology-free preservation of monuments," which he skillfully slipped in, mentioning the eliminated grave marker of the former Nazi functionary Wilhelm Gustloff, whom the schoolboy Konrad Pokriefke had planned to introduce in his second, also banned, presentation as a "great son of the city of Schwerin." For reasons of educational responsibility it had been necessary to prevent the spread of such dangerous nonsense, the more so because there was a growing number of boys and girls, in both schools, with radical right-wing tendencies. The East German teacher emphasized in his concluding remarks his school's "antifascist tradition," while all that occurred to the West German teacher was the fairly overused Ovid quotation, "Principiis obsta!—Beware the beginnings!"

All in all, the hearing of witnesses went smoothly, with the exception of Mother's outbursts, as well as those of the witness Rosi, who tearfully affirmed again and again that she would remain true to her "comrade, Konrad Pokriefke." Because proceedings in juvenile court are closed to the public, they were not held in chambers where effective speeches could be delivered. But then the presiding judge, who sometimes allowed himself little jokes, as if he wanted to introduce some levity into the deadly earnest background of this trial, gave my son an opportunity to illuminate the motivation for his deed, which Konny was all too glad to do, and at length, in an impromptu speech.

He began, of course, at the beginning, that is, with the birth of the later Landesgruppenleiter of the Nazi Party. Highlighting his organizational accomplishments in Switzerland and declaring his victory over tuberculosis "a victory of strength over weakness," he proceeded to sculpt a likeness of a hero. Thus he found an opportunity to celebrate, at long last, the "great son of the capital city of Schwerin." If the public had been admitted, approving murmurs might have been heard from the back rows.

When he reached the point where he dealt with the preparation and execution of the murder in Davos—Konrad soon abandoned his notes and quoted materials—he stressed the legal acquisition of the weapon and the number of shots that had been fired: "Like me, David Frankfurter scored four hits." My son also established a parallel to the motive that Frankfurter had articulated in the cantonal court, but expanded the statement: "I shot because I am a German—and because the eternal Jew spoke through David."

He passed quickly over the trial before the cantonal court in Chur, although he did say that he, in contrast to Professor Grimm and Party speaker Diewerge, did not believe Jewish instigators had been involved in the crime. For reasons of fairness, he added, it had to be said: like him, Frankfurter had acted "solely out of a personal sense of necessity."

After that Konrad offered a fairly vivid account of the state funeral rites in Schwerin, even providing information on the weather—"light snowfall"—and did not omit a single street name from his description of the parade. Then, after an excursus on the meaning, mission, and accomplishments of the NS organization Strength through Joy, which even the patient presiding judge found tiresome, he came to the laying of the ship's keel.

My son obviously enjoyed this portion of his speech to the court. Using his hands, he provided the statistics on the ship's length, breadth, and draft. And in connection with the launching and christening of the ship by the "martyr's widow," as he called her, he took the opportunity to exclaim reproachfully, "Here in Schwerin Frau Hedwig Gustloff's house was illegally expropriated after the collapse of the Greater German Reich, and later she was driven from the city!"

Then he began to speak of the inner life of the christened ship. He provided information on the reception and dining rooms, the number of cabins, the swimming pool on E deck. Finally he summarized, "The classless liner *Wilhelm Gustloff* was and remains the living expression of nationalist socialism, a model to this day, and truly exemplary for all times to come!"

It seemed to me that my son was listening to the applause of an imaginary audience after that last exclamation point; but at the same time he must have noticed the gaze of the judge, stern and warning him to cut it short. Relatively quickly, as Herr Stremplin might have said, Konny came to the final journey and the torpedoing of the ship. He characterized the appallingly large number of those who drowned and froze to death as a "rough estimate," and compared it to the far smaller number of victims of other ship sinkings. Then he gave the number of survivors, expressed gratitude to the captains, skipped over me, his father, completely, but mentioned his grandmother: "Present in this courtroom is seventy-year-old Ursula Pokriefke, in whose name I bear witness today," whereupon Mother stood up, white hair blazing and the fox around her neck, and took a bow. She, too, seemed to be appearing before a large audience.

As if Konny wanted to put an end to the applause audible only to him, he now assumed a very matter-of-fact tone, expressing appreciation for the "valuable attention to detail" manifested by the former purser's assistant Heinz Schön, and regret for the continuing destruction, during the postwar years, of the *Gustloff* wreck by divers searching for treasure: "But fortunately these barbarians found neither the Reichsbank gold nor the legendary amber room..."

At this point I thought I saw the all-too-patient judge nodding in agreement; but my son's speech sped on, as if under its own steam. Now he talked about the commander of the Soviet U-boat *S-13*. After his long imprisonment in Siberia, Aleksandr Marinesko had finally been rehabilitated. "Unfortunately he could enjoy the belated honor for only a short time. Not long after, he died of cancer..."

Not a single accusatory word. Nothing along the lines of what he had posted on the Internet about "subhuman Russians." On the contrary, my son surprised the judges and the juvenile magistrates, and probably even the prosecutor, by asking his murder victim Wolfgang Stremplin, as David, for forgiveness. For too long he had portrayed the sinking of the *Wilhelm Gustloff* on his Web site exclusively as a case of murder of women and children. Thanks to David, however, he had come to realize that the commander of *S-13* had properly considered the nameless ship a military target. "If there is any guilt to be assigned here," he exclaimed, "the supreme command of the navy, the admiral of the fleet must be indicted. He allowed a large number of military personnel to be put on board along with the refugees. The criminal here is Dönitz!"

Konrad paused, as if he had to wait for unrest and shouts in the courtroom to settle down. But perhaps he was searching for words with which to conclude. Finally he said, "I stand by my deed. But I ask the high court to recognize the execution I carried out as something that can be understood only in a larger context. I know: Wolfgang Stremplin was about to sit for his university qualifying exams. Unfortunately I could not take that into consideration. A matter of greater import was, and is, at stake. The regional capital Schwerin must honor its great son at long last. I call for the erection of a memorial on the southern bank of the lake, in the place where I honored the martyr's memory in my own way, a memorial that will remind us and coming generations of that Wilhelm Gustloff who was treacherously murdered by Jews. Just as the U-boat commander Aleksandr Marinesko was finally honored as a hero of the Soviet Union a few years ago with a monument in St. Petersburg, it is imperative that we honor a man who gave his life on 4 February 1936 so that Germany might finally be freed from the Jewish yoke. I do not hesitate to say that there are likewise reasons on the Jewish side to honor the medical student who gave a signal to his people with four shots—by means of a sculpture either in Israel, where David Frankfurter died at the age of eighty-two, or in Davos. Or just a bronze plaque, that would be okay too."

Finally the presiding judge pulled himself together: "That will do!" Silence settled over the courtroom. My son's explanations, or rather his outpouring, had not remained without effect; but his speech could not affect the severity or leniency of the finding, for the court must have recognized the coherent insanity floating in the flood of his speech, delusional notions that had been subject to more or less convincing analysis by experts.

On the whole I don't have much respect for this pseudo-scientific babble. But it's possible that one of the psychologists, a man who specialized in dysfunctional families, was not entirely off the mark when he attributed what he called Konny's "lonely act of desperation" to the defendant's growing up without a father, and dragged in my own fatherless origin and youth as a causative factor. The two other expert opinions pursued similar paths. Digging for dirt in the family backyard. In the end, the father is always to blame. Yet it was Gabi, with sole custody of the child, who did not stop him from moving from Mölln to Schwerin, where he ended up in Mother's clutches.

She, and she alone, is to blame. The witch with the fox stole around her neck. Always a will-o'-the-wisp, as a certain someone is well aware; he knew her from before, and I'm sure it was more than a casual acquaintance. Whenever he talks about Tulla...he gets all worked up...brings up mystical stuff...Some Kashubian or Koshavian water sprite, Thula, Duller, or Tul, is supposed to have been her godparent.

Her little head cocked, so that her stone-gray gaze lined up with the fox's glass eyes, Mother stared at the experts as they presented their findings. Sat there and listened unmoved as my failings as a father emerged as the pervasive theme of all the paper rustling—music to her ears. In the evaluations she appeared only in the margins. One assessment read, "The fundamentally well-intentioned care provided by the grandmother could not compensate for this at-risk youth's need for parental attention. It seems probable that the grand-mother's traumatic experiences, such as her survival of the disaster while pregnant, as well as her delivery in sight of the sinking ship, on the one hand made a pow-erful impression on her grandson Konrad Pokriefke, while on the other hand they had a disquieting effect be-cause of his powerful imaginative participation in these events..."

The defense attorney attempted to extend the line taken by the expert witnesses. This earnest man of my own age, hired by my ex, had not succeeded in gain-ing Konny's confidence. Whenever he spoke of an "un-premeditated, unintentional act," and attempted to downgrade the murder to mere manslaughter, my son negated all his defender's efforts by offering up volun-tary confessions: "I took my time and was perfectly calm. No, hate played no part in this. My thoughts were entirely practical. After the first shot to the stomach, which was aimed too low, I aimed the other three shots very carefully. Unfortunately with a pistol. I would have liked to have a revolver, like Frankfurter."

Konny presented himself as the responsible party. A gangly youth who had shot up too quickly, he stood there, with his glasses and curly hair, as his own accuser. He looked younger than seventeen but spoke as precociously as if he had taken a crash course in life. For instance, he refused to accept the notion that his parents shared his guilt. Smiling considerately, he said, "My mother is okay, even if she did get on my nerves with her constant harping on Auschwitz. And the court should quickly put my father out of its mind, as I've been doing for years—just forget him."

Did my son hate me? Was Konny even capable of hate? Several times he denied hating the Jews. I am inclined to speak of Konny's matter-of-fact hate. Hate turned down low. An eternal flame. A hate devoid of passion, reproducing itself asexually.

Or perhaps the defense attorney was not mistaken when he presented the fixation on Wilhelm Gustloff that Mother had caused as a search for a father substitute? He offered the fact that the Gustloffs had remained childless. To a needy Konrad Pokriefke, this discovery had offered a gap that could be filled virtually. The new technology, the Internet in particular, permitted such an escape from youthful loneliness.

It seemed to speak for the accuracy of this portrayal that when the judge allowed Konny to address this point, Konny spoke with enthusiasm, even warmth, of the "martyr." He said, "After my research revealed that Wilhelm Gustloff's commitment to societal change was influenced more by Gregor Strasser than by Hitler, I saw him as my sole model, which was expressed many times and unmistakably on my Web site. It is to the martyr that I owe my inner discipline. To avenge him was my sacred duty!"

When the prosecutor then questioned him quite insistently about the reasons for his despising the Jews, he said, "You have that all wrong. In theory I have nothing against the Jews. But like Wilhelm Gustloff, I hold the conviction that the Jew is a foreign body among the Aryan peoples. Let them all go to Israel, where they belong. Here they cannot be tolerated, and there they are urgently needed in the struggle against a hostile world around them. David Frankfurter was totally right when he made the decision to go to Palestine as soon as he was released. It was perfectly fitting that he found a job in the Israeli ministry of defense later."

In the course of the trial one could gain the impression that of all those who spoke, only my son was speaking his mind. He got to the point quickly, kept sight of the larger issues, had a solution for everything, and brought the case into focus, while the prosecution and the defense, the trinity of expert witnesses, as well as the presiding judge, the associate judges, and the juvenile magistrates were all groping around, searching for motives, invoking God and Freud as guides. They tried repeatedly to portray the "poor young man" as a victim of social circumstances—a failed marriage, a skewed school curriculum, and a godless world—and finally even to declare him guilty of "the genes passed down to Konrad from his grandmother, by way of his father," as my ex had the gall to theorize.

Next to nothing was said about the actual victim, the almost-graduate Wolfgang Stremplin, who had transformed himself online into the Jew David. He was left out of the picture in embarrassment, figuring only as a target. The defense attorney even suggested that he could be charged with provoking trouble by misrepresenting the facts. Although the idea that Stremplin had only himself to blame remained unspoken, it lurked behind casual remarks such as, "The victim veritably offered himself," or, "It was more than irresponsible to translate the Internet conflict into real life."

At any rate, the perpetrator received sizable doses of compassion. That probably explains why the Stremplins left town before the verdict was announced, but not before they had assured Gabi and me, in a cafe across from the courthouse, that they certainly did not want to see Konrad punished too harshly, and their son would no doubt have concurred. "We see ourselves as completely free of anything that might amount to a desire for revenge," Frau Stremplin said.

If I had been there simply on a professional basis, as a journalist, I would have criticized the reduced finding of manslaughter as "too lenient," if not as a "miscarriage of justice." As it was, leaving my obligation as a journalist aside and concentrating entirely on my son, who received his sentence of seven years in juvenile detention without emotion, I was horrified. Lost years! He will be twenty-four if he has to serve the entire time. The daily contact with criminals and genuine right-wingers will harden him, and once he is freed, he will presumably commit another crime and land in jail again. No! This verdict cannot be accepted.

But Konny refused to take advantage of the opportunity to appeal that his lawyer pointed out to him. I can only repeat what he is supposed to have said to Gabi: "Hard to believe that I got only seven years. They slapped eighteen years on the Jew Frankfurter, though of course he served only nine and a half..."

He didn't want to see me before he was taken away. And while still in the courtroom, he hugged not his mother but his grandmother, who reached only to his chest, even in her spike heels. When he had to go, he glanced around one more time; perhaps he was looking for David's or Wolfgang's parents and realized they were missing.

When we found ourselves standing outside the regional courthouse on Dremmlerplatz, and I could finally light up a cigarette, it turned out that Mother was furious. She had taken off the fox, and with that neck decoration for official occasions she had also dropped her stilted High German: "You can't call that justice!" Furiously she ripped the cigarette out of my mouth and stomped on it, as a substitute for something else she wanted to destroy, yelled for a while, and then talked herself into a frenzy: "That's a crime! There's no justice anymore. They should've nailed me, not the boy. No, no,

I was the one who gave him that computer thinga-mabob, and then gave him that gun last Easter, because they personally threatened my Konradchen, them skin-heads. One time he came home bleeding—they'd beaten him up. But he didn't cry, not one bit. No, no. I had that in my drawer for ages. Bought it right after the changeover at the Russki mart. Real cheap. But in court not a soul asked me where the thing came from . . ."

9

THE DO NOT ENTER SIGN HE POSTED AT THE VERY beginning. He strictly enjoined me from speculating about Konny's thoughts, from creating scenarios based on what he might be thinking, perhaps even writing down what might be going on in his head and presenting it as suitable for quoting.

He said, "No one knows what he was thinking and is thinking now. Every mind is sealed, not just his. A no-man's-land for word hunters. No point to opening up the skull. Besides, no one says out loud what he thinks. And anyone who tries to is already lying in the first words that come out. Sentences starting with 'At that moment he was thinking...' have never been anything but crutches. Nothing is locked tighter than a mind. Even progressively harsher torture doesn't produce complete confessions. Even in the moment of death, a person can cheat in his thoughts. That's why we can't know what Wolfgang Stremplin was thinking when the decision to play the Jew David on the Internet was ripening within him, or what literally was going on in his head as he stood in front of the Kurt Bürger Youth Hostel and saw his bosom enemy, who had called himself Wilhelm on line, and now, as Konrad Pokriefke, pulled a pistol from the right pocket of his parka and after the first shot to the stomach fired three more shots that hit his head and its sealed-in thoughts. We see only what we see. The surface doesn't tell everything, but enough. So no thoughts, including none thought out ex post facto. If we use words sparingly, we'll get to the end more quickly."

It's a good thing he can't guess the thoughts that against my will come creeping out of the left and right hemispheres of my brain, making terrible sense, revealing anxiously guarded secrets, exposing me, so that I am horrified, and quickly try to think about something else. For instance, I thought about a gift I could bring my son in Neustrelitz, something to show I cared, suitable for my first visit.

Since I had had all the newspaper coverage of the trial sent to me by a clipping service, I had in my possession a photo of Wolfgang Stremplin that appeared in the *Badische Zeitung*. He looked nice, but not distinctive. A boy about to leave school for the university, perhaps, certainly old enough for military service. While his mouth smiled, his eyes had a slightly mournful expression. He wore his dark-blond hair unparted and slightly wavy. A young man whose head tilted to the left above his open collar. Possibly an idealist, thinking who knows what.

I might add that the press coverage of my son's trial was disappointingly slim. Around the time of the proceedings, both parts of the now united Germany were experiencing a series of right-wing extremist criminal acts, among them the attempted killing of a Hungarian in Potsdam with baseball bats and the beating of a retiree in Bochum that led to his death. Skinheads were striking everywhere, relentlessly. Politically motivated violence had come to seem routine, likewise appeals addressed to the right and expressions of regret by politicians who supplied those committing acts of violence with tinder, concealed in asides. But perhaps it was the undeniable fact that Wolfgang Stremplin was not a Jew that diminished interest in the trial, for initially, right after the deed, there had been banner headlines all over the country: JEWISH FELLOW CITIZEN SHOT! and COWARDLY MURDER MOTIVATED BY ANTI-SEMITISM! The caption to the photo of Wolfgang echoed this sensationalism: "The victim of the most recent act of anti-Semitic violence." I snipped off this caption.

So when I paid my first visit to the juvenile detention center—a pretty run-down place that seemed ripe for demolition—I had the newspaper photo of Wolfgang Stremplin tucked into my breast pocket. Konny even thanked me when I pushed the piece of newsprint, folded only once, toward him. He smoothed it with his hand, and smiled. Our conversation dragged, but at least he was speaking to me. In the visitation room we sat opposite each other; at other tables other juvenile detainees also had visitors.

Since I have been forbidden to try to read my son's thoughts from his forehead, all that remains to be said is that face-to-face with his father he was closemouthed as always, but did not give me the cold shoulder. He even favored me with a question about my journalistic work. When I told him about a story I was doing on Dolly, the miracle sheep cloned in Scotland, and her creator, I saw him smile. "Mama will certainly be interested in that. She's fascinated by genes, especially mine."

Then I heard about the option of playing Ping-Pong in the recreation area, and learned that he shared a cell with three other youths—"pretty screwed-up, but harmless." He had his own corner, with a table and bookshelf. Distance learning was also available. "That'll be something new!" he exclaimed. "I'll do my university qualifying exams behind prison walls, proctored indefinitely, so to speak." I didn't particularly like to see Konny attempting to be witty.

When I left, I saw his girlfriend Rosi waiting to take my place. She looked as though she had been crying, and was dressed all in black, as if in mourning. A general coming and going was characteristic of visiting day: sobbing mothers, embarrassed fathers. The guard who checked the gifts fairly casually allowed me to bring in the photo of Wolfgang as David. Before me, Mother had no doubt already been there, perhaps with Gabi; or had the two visited Konny one after the other?

Time passed. I was no longer feeding Dolly the miracle sheep with high-cellulose-content paper, but was hot on the heels of other sensational stories. Meanwhile one of my short-lived relationships—this time it was with a photographer who specialized in cloud formations—

happened to come to an end, without any hue and cry. Then another visiting day was marked on the calendar.

We had hardly sat down facing each other when my son told me that he had made frames for several photos, which he now had behind glass and mounted under his bookshelf: "The one of David, too, of course." He had also framed two photos that had been part of his Web site material; Mother must have brought them at his request. They were two images of Captain Third Class Aleksandr Marinesko, which, however, as my son said, could not have been more different. He had fished the images out of the Internet. Two Marinesko fans had claimed separately that they had the true likeness in their frames. "A comical quarrel," Konny said, and pulled the two pictures, like family photos, out from under his indestructible Norwegian sweater.

He lectured me in a factual tone: "The round-faced one next to the periscope is on display at the St. Petersburg Naval Museum. This one here, with the angular face, standing in the tower of his boat, is supposed to be the real Marinesko. At any rate, there's written evidence indicating that the original of this photo was given to a Finnish whore who serviced Marinesko regularly. Marinesko had a thing for women, as we know. Interesting to see what kind of traces a person like that leaves..."

My son talked for a long time about his little picture gallery, which included an early and a late photograph of David Frankfurter; the late one showed him as an old man and relapsed smoker. One picture was missing. I was already feeling somewhat hopeful when Konny, as if he could read his father's thoughts, gave me to understand that the detention center's administration had unfortunately forbidden him to adorn the wall of his cell with his "really cool picture of the martyr in uniform."

Mother was his most frequent visitor, or at least she came more often than I did. Gabi was usually too busy with "teachers' union stuff" to get away; she's thrown herself into the committee studying "Research on Child Rearing," on a voluntary basis, of course. Not to forget Rosi: she visited fairly regularly, soon no longer looking tearful.

In the current year I was taken up with the election hysteria, which broke out early and throughout the Federal Republic. Like the rest of the media hyenas, I was trying to read the entrails of the nonstop polls; content-wise, they had little to offer. What did become clear was that the Christian Democrat Pastor Hintze with his "Red Sock Campaign" would give the Party of German Socialists, successor to the East German Socialist Unity Party, a black eye, but he could not save the fat man, who ended up losing the election. I traveled a lot, interviewing Bundestag members, mid-level big shots in business, even some *Republikaner,* for the forecasts suggested that this right-wing party would gain more than the five percent needed for Bundestag representation. It was particularly active in Mecklenburg-Vorpommern, if with only moderate success.

I did not get to Neustrelitz, but I learned from a telephone conversation with Mother that her "Konradchen" was thriving. He had even gained "a couple pounds." He had also been "promoted," as she put it, to instructor of a computing course for young delinquents. "Well, you know, he always was a whizz at that kind of stuff..."

So I pictured my son, now with chubby cheeks, teaching his fellow prisoners the ABCs of the latest software, although I assumed that the inmates at the detention center would not be allowed to connect to the Internet; otherwise some of them would be able, under the guidance of Konrad Pokriefke, to find a virtual escape route: a collective jailbreak into cyberspace.

I also learned that a Neustrelitz Ping-Pong team to which my son belonged had played a team from the Plötzensee detention center, and won. To sum up: this journalist's son, who had been convicted of manslaughter and had meanwhile come of age, was busy around the clock. In early summer he passed his university qualifying examinations by correspondence, receiving the excellent score of 1.6; I sent a telegram: "Congratulations, Konny!"

And then I heard from Mother: she had been in Polish Gdańsk for more than a week. When I visited her back in Schwerin, this was her account: "Course I also ran around in Danzig, but mostly I spent my time in Langfuhr. It's all changed. But the house on Elsenstrasse's still standing. Even the balconies with flower boxes are still there..."

She'd signed up for a bus tour. "Real reasonable it was for us!" A group of expellees, women and men of Mother's age, had responded to an ad put out by a travel agency that organized "nostalgia tours." Mother commented, "It was nice there. You've got to give the Polacks credit—they've rebuilt a whole lot, all the churches and such. Except the statue of Gutenberg—we kids used to call him Kuddenpäch, and it was in the Jäschkental Woods, right behind the Erbsberg—it's not there anymore. But in Brösen—I used to go there in good weather—there's a real nice beach, just like there used to be..."

Then her I'm-not-home look. But soon the broken record started up again: the way it used to be long ago, even longer ago, long, long ago, in the courtyard of the carpentry shop, or the way they'd built a snowman in the woods, or what went on during the summer holidays at the Baltic shore, "when I was skinny as a rail..." With a bunch of boys she had swum out to a shipwreck, whose superstructure had stuck up out of the water since the beginning of the war. "We'd dive way, way down into that old rusty crate. And one of the boys, the one who went in the deepest, he was called Jochen..."

I forgot to ask Mother whether she'd taken her fox along on the nostalgia tour, in spite of the summer weather. But I did ask whether Aunt Jenny had gone with her to Danzig-Langfuhr and other places. "Nah," Mother said, "she didn't want to go, 'cause of her legs, and what have you. Too painful, she said it'd be. But the route we used to take to school, me and my girlfriend, I walked it a couple of times. It felt much shorter than it used to..."

Mother must have served other travel impressions,

piping hot, to my son, including all the details of what she confessed to me, in a whisper: "I was in Gotenhafen, too, by myself. Right where they put us on board. In my mind I pictured the whole thing, all those little kids, head down in the icy water. Wanted to cry, but I couldn't…" Again that I'm-not-home look. And then the KDF refrain: "That was one beautiful ship…"

Accordingly I was not surprised that on my next visit in Neustrelitz, right after the elections, I was confronted with a piece of obsessive handiwork. The construction kit my son had used was a gift, no doubt paid for out of Mother's pocketbook.

You find things like this in the toy section of large department stores, where they have shelves and shelves of neatly organized models, representing famous originals that fly, drive, or float. I doubt she found it in Schwerin. She probably went looking in Hamburg in the Alsterhaus or in Berlin at KdW, the Kaufhaus des Westens, and found what she wanted. She got to Berlin often. These days she was driving a VW Golf and was on the road a lot. She was a terror behind the wheel, passing other cars as a matter of principle.

When she came to Berlin, it wasn't to visit me in my messy bachelor pad in Kreuzberg but to "chew the fat" in Schmargendorf with her old girlfriend Jenny, eating pastry and drinking Red Riding Hood champagne. Since the changeover, the two of them saw each other often, as if they had to compensate for time lost after the Wall went up. They made a strange pair.

When Mother visited Aunt Jenny—on the occasions when I was allowed to sit in—she acted bashful, as if she were still a little girl who had just played a mean trick on Jenny and now wanted to undo the damage. Aunt Jenny, on the other hand, seemed to have forgiven her for all the awful things she did to her long ago. I saw her stroke Mother's head as Mother hobbled past her, whispering, "It's all right, Tulla, it's all right." Then the two of them fell silent. And Aunt Jenny sipped her hot lemonade. Aside from Konrad, who had drowned while swimming, and Konny, who had committed a crime, if there was anyone else Mother loved, it was her old school friend.

Since the days when I had occupied that little room in the Schmargendorf apartment under the eaves, not a single piece of furniture has been moved. All the knick-knacks standing about, yet not covered with dust, looked like survivals from yesteryear. And just as all the walls at Aunt Jenny's, even the sloping ones, are plastered with ballet photos—Aunt Jenny, who became known under the *nom d'artiste* of Angustri, sylphlike as Giselle, in *Swan Lake* and *Coppelia,* solo or posing next to her equally delicate ballet master—Mother too is plastered inside and out with memories. And if people can trade memories, as the expression goes, Karlsbader Strasse was and is the trading floor for these durable goods.

So on one of these trips to Berlin—before or after her visit to Aunt Jenny—she must have picked out a very special model from the assortment at KdW. Not the

Dornier hydroplane *Do X,* not a King Tiger tank model, not the battleship *Bismarck,* which was sunk as early as '41, or the heavy cruiser *Admiral Hipper,* which was junked after the war, seemed suitable as a present. It was not something military she selected; it was the passenger vessel *Wilhelm Gustloff* on which she had her heart set. I doubt she let any salesclerk help her; Mother has always known what she wants.

My son must have been given special permission to show off this particular object in the visiting room. At any rate, the guard on duty nodded benevolently when the inmate Konrad arrived, loaded down with the model ship. The sight started a reel of thoughts unwinding in me that soon formed an impenetrable tangle. Is this never going to end? Must this story keep repeating itself? Can't Mother get over it? What in the world was she thinking of?

To Konny, now of age, I said, "That's very nice. But aren't you too old for this kind of thing now?" He admitted that I had a point. "I know. But if you'd given me the *Gustloff* for my birthday when I was thirteen or fourteen, I wouldn't have to make up for missing out on this kid's stuff. I had fun doing it, though. And I have plenty of time, right?"

The reproach hit home. And while I was still trying to recover, asking myself whether playing with the damned ship as a model, while he was still a boy and also under his father's supervision, might have averted the worst, he said, "I asked Grandma Tulla to get it for me. I wanted to see with my own eyes how the ship looked. Came out pretty well, didn't it?"

From stem to stern, the Strength through Joy ship showed itself in all its beauty. From the thousands of parts my son had fashioned the vacationer's classless dream boat. How spacious the sundeck was, not chopped up by any superstructures! How elegantly the single funnel rose amidships, slightly inclined toward the stern! Clearly recognizable the glassed-in promenade deck! Beneath the bridge the winter garden, known as the Bower. I considered where inside the ship the E deck with the swimming pool might be, and counted the lifeboats: none was missing.

Konny had placed the gleaming white model in a wire rack of his own devising. The hull was visible down to the keel. I expressed my admiration, though with a touch of irony, for the skillful hobbyist. He reacted to my praise with laughter that was more a giggle, then whipped out of his pocket a little tin that had once held peppermint drops and in which he now had three red paste-on dots, about the size of a pfennig. With the three dots he marked the places in the hull where the torpedoes hit their mark: one dot on the port side of the forecastle, the next on the spot where I had guessed the swimming pool must be, the third at the location of the engine room. Konrad performed this task solemnly. After applying these stigmata to the ship's body, he stepped back to observe the effect, was apparently satisfied, and said, "Nice work." Then he abruptly changed the subject.

My son wanted to know how I had voted in the election. I said, "Certainly not for the *Republikaner*," and then admitted that it had been years since I'd gone near a polling place. "That's typical of you, not to have any real convictions," he said, but wouldn't reveal how he had voted on his mail-in ballot. Suspecting Mother's influence, I guessed that he might have gone for the PDS. But he merely smiled, and then began to fasten to the model ship small flags, which he had apparently made himself and which had been waiting in another little tin, to be affixed to the bow, the stern, and the tops of the two masts. He had even produced miniature versions of the KDF emblem and the flag of the German Labor Front, nor was the one with the swastika missing. The fully dressed ship. Everything was just right, but with him nothing was right.

What can be done when a son takes possession of his father's thoughts, thoughts that have been festering for years under a lid, and even translates them into action? All my life I have tried to take the right tack, at least politically, not to say the wrong thing, to appear correct on the outside. That's called self-discipline. Whether for the Springer papers or the *Tageszeitung,* I always sang along. Even had myself convinced by the stuff I turned out. Whipping up hatred, cynically slinging the lingo—two courses of action I practiced alternately without any difficulty. But I never took the lead, never set the direction in editorials. Others picked the topics. I steered a middle course, never slid all the way to the right or the left, didn't cause any collisions, swam with the current, let myself drift, kept my head above water. Well, that probably had to do with the circumstances of my birth; that could explain almost everything.

But then my son kicked up a storm. No surprise, actually. Was bound to happen. After everything Konny had posted on the Internet, blathered in the chat room, proclaimed on his Web site, those carefully aimed shots fired on the southern bank of Lake Schwerin were absolutely consistent. Now he was locked up, had gained respect by winning at Ping-Pong and running a computing course, could boast of passing his exams with flying colors, and, as Mother had shared with me, was already receiving job offers from businesses for later on: the new technologies! He seemed to have a future in the new century that was just around the bend. He made a cheerful impression, looked well fed, and talked fairly rationally, but was still waving the flag—in the form of a miniature. This will end badly, I thought confusedly, and went looking for advice.

First, because I was really at a loss, I even went to Aunt Jenny. The old lady in her doll's house sat there, her head trembling slightly, and listened to everything I came out with, more or less honestly. You could unload with her. She was used to this, presumably since her youth. After I had dumped most of the tangle at her feet, she presented me with her frozen smile and said, "It's the evil that needs to come out. My old girlfriend, your dear mother, knows this problem well. Dear me, when I think how I used to suffer as a little girl when she had those outbursts. And my adoptive father, too—I'm supposed to be the child of real Gypsies, which had to be kept secret in those days—well, that rather eccentric schoolteacher, whose name, Brunies, I was allowed to take, got to know Tulla from her evil side. It was pure mischief on her part. But it turned out badly. After the denunciation, they came for Papa Brunies... He was sent to Stutthof... But in the end things turned out almost all right. You should talk to her about your worries. Tulla knows from her own experience how completely a person can change..."

So I took A24 and floored the pedal to the Schwerin exit. Yes, I talked to Mother, to the extent it was possible to share with her these thoughts of mine that were scuttling this way and that. We sat on the balcony of her eleventh-floor apartment in the renovated concrete-slab building on Gagarinstrasse, with its view of the broadcast tower; down below, Lenin was still standing, gazing westward. Her place seemed unchanged, but recently Mother had rediscovered the faith of her youth. She was playing the Catholic and had set up a sort of home altar in one corner of the living room, where, between candles and plastic flowers—white lilies—a small picture of the Blessed Virgin was displayed; the photo next to it, showing Comrade Stalin in dress whites and genially smoking a pipe, made an odd impression. It was difficult to stare at this altar and not make some remark.

I had brought honey squares and poppy-seed bars, which I knew Mother liked. When I had spilled my guts, she said, "You needn't worry too much about our

Konradchen. He's paying for what he got himself into. And when he's free again, I'm sure he'll be a genuine radical, like I used to be when my own comrades gave me a hard time for being Stalin's last faithful follower. No, you won't see any more bad things happening to him. Our Konradchen's always had a guardian angel hovering over him..."

She displayed "bashed-in windows," then resumed her normal expression and confirmed what her friend Jenny with unfailing instinct had said: "The stuff we have in our heads and everywhere, all that evil has to come out..."

No, Mother had no helpful advice for me. Her white-haired ideas were shorn too close. But where else could I go? To Gabi, by any chance?

Once more I took the beaten path from Schwerin to Mölln, and, as always happened, was struck by the unpretentious beauty of the town, which, going back in history, invokes Till Eulenspiegel, but could hardly stand his pranks today. Because my ex had recently acquired a live-in boyfriend, a "dear, gentle person, easily hurt," as she said, we met in nearby Ratzeburg and ate at the Seehof, with a view of swans and ducks, among them an indefatigable diving duck. She ordered vegetarian, and I had the Wiener schnitzel.

She led with the statement, "God knows, I don't want to hurt your feelings," then proceeded to blame me for everything that had gone wrong with our son. Finally she said, "You know, I haven't been able to get anywhere with the boy for a long time now. He shuts himself off. He's not receptive to love and that kind of attention. Lately I've reached the conclusion that deep inside him, and that includes his innermost thoughts, everything's ruined. But when I take your mother into consideration, I get a sense of what she passed on to her own fine son and from him to Konrad. That can't be changed. By the way, on my last visit your son broke off all contact with me."

Then she gave me to understand that she wanted to start a new life with her "warmhearted yet smart and sophisticated" partner. She deserved this "modest opportunity" after everything she had been through. "And just think, Paul: at last I've found the strength to stop smoking." We skipped dessert. Out of consideration for her I refrained from lighting up another cigarette. My ex insisted on paying for her own meal.

In retrospect, my attempt to get advice from Rosi, my son's devoted girlfriend, strikes me as ludicrous, but also revealing of what the future held. The very next day, which was visiting day, we met at a cafe in Neustrelitz, shortly after she had seen Konny. Her eyes were no longer red. Her hair, which before had fallen loose to her shoulders, was now pinned up in a neat bun. Her posture, previously self-abnegating, had stiffened. Even her hands, which before had moved restlessly, as though searching for something to hold on to, now rested on the table, firmly clenched. She assured me, "How you choose to conduct yourself as a father is up to you. As for me, I'll always believe in the good in Konny, no matter what. He's so strong, such a model of strength. And I'm not the only one who believes in him firmly, absolutely firmly—and not only in thoughts."

I told her she was right about his good core. Theoretically that was my belief, too. I wanted to say more, but she said, as if to bring the conversation to a close, "It's not him but the world that's evil." The moment had come for me to announce my visit at the juvenile detention center.

For the first time I was allowed to visit him in his cell. Apparently Konrad Pokriefke had won this onetime special privilege as a reward for good behavior and exemplary social conduct. His fellow inmates were outdoors, I heard, working in the gardens. Konny was waiting for me in the corner he called his own.

It was an old dump, this facility, but word had it that a modern replacement was in the works. On the one hand I thought I was immune to surprises by now, on the other I was afraid of my son's sudden inspirations.

As I entered and at first saw only stained walls, he was sitting in his Norwegian sweater at a table shoved against the wall, and said, without looking up, "Well, Dad?"

With a casual gesture. My son, who had caught me unawares with his "Dad," indicated the bookshelf, where all the framed photos were gone, removed from the wall—those of David as Wolfgang, Frankfurter young and old, the two purported images of the U-boat commander Marinesko. Nothing new had taken their place. I ran a quick eye over the spines of the books on the shelf: what one might expect—a lot of history, some works on the new technologies, in their midst two volumes of Kafka.

I did not comment on the vanished photos. And he didn't seem to have expected any comment. What happened next went quickly. Konrad stood up, lifted from its wire rack in the middle of the table the model of the ship named for Wilhelm Gustloff and marked with three red dots. He leaned the ship against the rack as if it were listing, and then began, not in haste or in anger, but rather with premeditated deliberateness, to smash with his bare fist his carefully pieced-together creation.

That must have hurt. After four or five blows, the side of his right fist began to bleed. He had probably cut himself on the funnel, the lifeboats, the two masts. But he kept going. When the hull refused to give way beneath his blows, he picked up the wreck in both hands, swung it to one side, raised it to eye level, and then let it fall to the floor, which was made of oiled planks. He then trampled what was left of the model *Wilhelm Gustloff,* the last thing being the remaining lifeboats, which had popped out of their davits.

"Satisfied now, Dad?" After that, not a word. His gaze went to the barred window, and remained fixed on it. I babbled something, I no longer recall what. Something positive. "Never give up," or, "Let's make a fresh start together," or some such rubbish from American movies: "I'm proud of you, son." When I left, my son had nothing more to say.

A few days later, no, the next day, someone—the

same someone in whose name I have been doing this crabwalk and making some progress—urged me to go online. He said the mouse might lead me to a suitable conclusion. Until then I'd practiced restraint: only what I needed professionally, occasional porno, that was it. Since Konny had been locked up, the ether was silent. And David was gone, of course.

I had to surf for a long time. The name of the accursed ship appeared on the screen numerous times, but nothing new, nothing final and conclusive. Then it turned out to be worse than I had feared. At the URL www.kameradschaft-konrad-pokriefke.de, a Web site introduced itself in German and English, campaigning for someone whose conduct and thinking it held up as exemplary, someone whom the hated system had for that very reason locked up. "We believe in you, we will wait for you, we will follow you..." And so on and so forth.

It doesn't end. Never will it end.